of the
date

CARDINAL OBSESSION

By the same author

Design for Murder
Dead Ringer
Breaths of Suspicion
A Fugitive Englishman

The Arnold Landon Novels

Shadowmaker
Dragonhead
Grave Error
Headhunter
The Ways of Death
Dead Secret
An Assumption of Death
The Ghost Dancers
The Shape Shifter
Suddenly as a Shadow
Angel of Death
A Short-Lived Ghost
The Cross Bearer
Bloodeagle
A Wisp of Smoke
The Devil is Dead
Men of Subtle Craft
A Trout in the Milk
Most Cunning Workmen
A Gathering of Ghosts
Goddess of Death

CARDINAL
OBSESSION

ROY LEWIS

ROBERT HALE · LONDON

Robert Hale Limited
Clerkenwell House
Clerkenwell Green
London EC1R 0HT

www.halebooks.com

Typeset in Palatino
Printed in Great Britain by Berforts Information Press Ltd

PROLOGUE

THEY HAD SOMETIMES called him *Il Moro*, because of his dark, swarthy complexion, but that had been when he was a child and unable to respond to the insult: matters had changed, with the vicious power that he could now unleash upon his enemies.

It was many years now since he had heard the sobriquet: few dared use the sneering reference for he was now Duke of Milan, the Eagle, the powerful and respected Lodovico Sforza.

Powerful, respected and ruthless. Naturally, his enemies – and there were many of them – might still call him *Il Moro* behind his back but they knew his reputation; they hated him for his ambitions, then for his political intrigues, not least his manoeuvrings with the French king. It was a hatred that only increased when that monarch had shown his own greed for power in Milan and the Duke was forced to change his search for allies. Lodovico's volte-face in his creation of an alliance with Maximilian I, the Holy Roman Emperor, had caused his enemies to rage impotently. As for his acquisition of the Dukedom of Milan, there were some who whispered that it was Lodovico himself who was behind the mysterious death of his own nephew, a death that had opened the road to the

dukedom for himself. In his position of power, he could afford
to ignore such whispers.

But there was another side to the personality of *Il Moro*:
he had built up a reputation as a man widely-read, an
accomplished linguist, patron of the arts and, urged by the
promptings of his young wife Beatrice, the man who had
commissioned Leonardo da Vinci's magnificent painting of
The Last Supper. Indeed, the Duke of Milan continued to act as
patron to the accomplished and almost legendary Leonardo da
Vinci, the man who not only designed engines of destruction,
but who had orchestrated Lodovico's wedding celebrations
some years ago....

But the duke's adored wife Beatrice was sadly no more.

Lodovico stared blankly at the pages in front of him: he
had been working on them for some hours and now, in the
flickering candlelight, he was tired. He frowned as the image
of Beatrice came to his mind. He had loved her well and she
had proved to be a model wife, but he was a virile man and
there had of course been mistresses. There was Cecilia, who
had borne him a son, Lucrezia on whom he had fathered two
children. Beatrice had understood; he was a lusty man in his
prime and he needed to expend his sexual energies with more
than one woman. And now, as he wrestled with the political
problems enunciated in the documents that lay before him,
other thoughts began to dance in his head, the need to return
in triumph to Milan, the machinations required to bind closely
to him the princes who would support him in his bid to throw
out the hated French from his dukedom, but his loins stirred,
not only at the memory of Beatrice but also at the thought that
the time of his romantic assignation this night was now close.

Impatiently, he thrust aside the pile of papers and rose to
his feet. The woman he was expecting in his private chambers

was named Carlotta Fantini. He had seen her only once, when she had been pointed out to him in the Hall of Princes; a tall, golden-haired woman with a superb body and bold eyes. Her reputation had preceded her on her arrival in Padua. She was reckoned to be a princess among courtesans and the glance she had bestowed upon him had told him that if he wished, she would be available.

He had made arrangements that very day. One of his minions had quietly approached Carlotta in her own palazzo; he reported back to the duke that the woman would be delighted to make his closer acquaintance. The assignation had been made, but now she was late.

He frowned. Lodovico Sforza was a man of precise and controlled habits. He devoted his daylight hours to the solution of problems, the dealing with the political demands upon his time, the necessary machinations with princes and the Pope. But with the descending twilight his thoughts turned away from the papers on his desk. A few moments ago, somewhere in the city, a bell had sounded the hour. It meant that Carlotta Fantini would be on her way to his apartments, for the agreed assignation. Indeed, she should be here by now. He had cast aside his work for the evening, dismissed his courtiers and now awaited the woman.

But it seemed she was late. The realization angered him; he was the Duke of Milan. She was a mere courtesan, lovely and desirable though she might be. He would make her pay for her carelessness. The thought of what he might do to her body, by way of penance, made his loins stir again.

He caught the sound of a muffled cry from the anteroom to his apartment. He hesitated, then with mounting anger he strode towards the door. She had arrived, but some fool of a courtier must be preventing her entrance. He was impatient, the idiot who was intervening in the pursuit of the duke's pleasures would be made to feel the whip and more. His right hand instinctively grasped the hilt of the poniard that he wore at his belt as thoughts of violence intruded upon his lust.

He threw open the door.

The sight that greeted him riveted him to the spot for a moment. He had expected to see the woman, Carlotta – and perhaps a panicked clerk. The room was shadowy and he made out the form of the woman he was expecting, but she was not accompanied by a courtier. Instead he could make out the forms of five men. And no one he recognized as a member of his entourage.

Two of the strangers in the anteroom were holding her by the arms as she struggled frantically; a third had clasped his hands about her mouth to stifle her anguished cries. His mind registered briefly that her dress was torn, her breast exposed. He also glimpsed the dark stain of blood at her waist. The other two men stared at the duke, frozen, perhaps momentarily confused by Ludovico Sforza's sudden appearance in the doorway. But their reaction was momentary only. As he stood there, shocked in the open doorway, they were the first to recover. The two men regained their composure and their intentions; they were now rushing towards him. Both men were armed and he saw the glitter of blades as they came for him.

The Duke of Milan was physically strong and no coward, and he had many times distinguished himself in battles. Moreover, he was a man of headstrong capabilities and the sight of the men rushing at him, and that of the woman struggling for her freedom and, perhaps his life, brought a black rage upon him.

He roared a curse and rather than retreat from their attack

he flung himself upon his assailants, holding aloft his own poniard as he did so. They were astonished; they had probably expected that he would try to flee back into his chambers and the sudden eruption of his attack caught them at a disadvantage. His blade flickered in the dim light as he slashed the throat of the nearest man in one swift movement. The blade sliced home and the mortally injured assassin, choking on his own blood, staggered sideways into his companion, knocking him off balance. Then almost in the same movement the duke was thrusting at his second assailant. The man threw up an arm to protect his throat and slashed wildly, driving his own blade at the duke, but Sforza was an accomplished fighter; he sidestepped the assassin's blade and his own knife plunged into the man's exposed stomach.

The duke's blood was up, he was roaring in violent rage. He was shouting loudly and it seemed to unnerve the three men holding Carlotta Fantini. He – and they – knew that in a matter of moments the alarm would be raised and his personal guards would storm into the room. But in the meantime he was rushing upon them in his blood-spattered clothing and the men scattered, whirling the courtesan across the room, away from them and the enraged ruler of Milan. She collided with a small table, and collapsed in a half-fainting fit to the floor. The duke threw himself forward in mad blood lust.

Sforza did not know how these men would have gained entrance to his apartments. He knew there must have been bribery involved and even in his blind rage, he swore that in due course he would find out who had betrayed him and the culprits would pay with their lives. He doubted that Carlotta herself would have been involved, for she was injured and still sprawled in a swoon on the floor but as he dashed forward he realized that though the swift turn of events might have caught the assassins off balance, they were still dangerous and intent upon assassination. One man stood over Carlotta Fantini, as though uncertain what to do; he was out of the immediate range of the duke's fury. But the other two were half-crouched, blades at the ready as he rushed upon them. It would be an uneven struggle but Ludovico Sforza had no thought for the danger he was in; he was beside himself, and his wild advance seemed to alarm his assailants momentarily. But even as he threw himself upon the taller of the two assassins, he became aware of a violent hammering at the door, and moments later it burst open. Immediately the situation had changed.

Now, the guards were rushing in and the three assassins sought frantically to escape the trap they had created for themselves.

The skirmish was brief. Sword blades glittered in the pale, flickering candlelight; two of the assailants had been cornered, but the third, giving up all thoughts of assassination, had rushed past Sforza and dashed into the bedchamber, slamming the door shut behind him. The Duke of Milan hesitated, thought about pursuit and then glanced at the courtesan he had been expecting to enliven his evening. He waved to the guards, ordered them to corner the remaining assassin – the other two were already bleeding out their lives on the floor of the anteroom – and he bent over Carlotta, raising her from the floor where she was still half-conscious. Her wound was not serious, but the sight of her blood inflamed his passions even further.

He laid her down. The guards had already put two of the assassins to the sword, though one clearly still lived, but the duke wanted to corner the last man, to question him, on the rack and under the hot iron.

Sforza turned and raged back to his bedchamber, poniard in

hand. The door held against him but he stormed at it with his shoulder; three blows and it gave way and he roared into the chamber, seeking the final assassin with his guards at his back.

The room was empty. A curtain lifted in the night breeze. The window was open and as Sforza leaned out he could see the red-tiled roofs of the palace stretching below him. After a moment, as his eyes became accustomed to the dark, he was able to make out a dark figure frantically scrambling across the tiles, about to drop into the courtyard below.

Lodovico Sforza bellowed to his guards. The man must be hunted down. He and his brother assassins had obtained entry to the ducal apartments. Lodovico Sforza must discover who had been bribed, who had allowed them entry, who had backed them with gold to attack the Duke of Milan. He needed to know who, among his many enemies, had launched this attack.

He called for two of the guards to bring the unconscious Carlotta to his bed. He looked at her carefully as she lay there. She was indeed beautiful, and the wound was superficial. There would be another day … or why not tonight? He leaned over her; her eyelids fluttered, she had magnificent eyes, and she managed a weak smile. A magnificent woman....

He himself was unhurt. The attempted assassination had failed. The Duke of Milan had triumphed and heads would roll – after the rack and other implements had played their part on the bodies of the culprits who remained alive.

Sforza took a deep breath, his anger receding as the adrenalin of triumph swept through his veins. He turned then, as he looked about him, some of that surge of triumph receded. He stared at the night table beside the bed, the damasked wall where his prized possession had hung. The wall and table had been swept clean.

One of the assassins had fled rather than fought, but he had not left empty-handed as he jumped from the window to the tiles.

And the Eagle had been taken.

The Duke of Milan clenched his fist. The two men apprehended by his guards would be racked, even though already dying, and they would feel the heat of the irons before they talked. And as for the fugitive who had escaped over the tiles … there would be no part of Italy that he would be able to hide. The manhunt would begin this night.

Meanwhile, Carlotta Fantini lay there, weak, surrendered, unable to resist. The duke strode to the door, flung it open, bawled for his guards and issued his orders. They would seek the fugitive. They would find the last assassin. They would bring him to the duke, for the iron and the rack. And they would recover the Eagle.

But while they began their search of Padua he needed to slake the fury and the heat in his loins.

Carlotta Fantini would not resist.

And the blood staining her dress served only to stimulate his desire....

CHAPTER ONE

Paul Gilbert completed the photographing of the statuary that had caught his interest about five o'clock in the afternoon. He spent the next half hour gathering up his equipment before taking one more look around the museum at Chesters Fort. He pondered for a while over the ancient commemorative stone that proclaimed the pride felt by the men of the Tenth Legion at their completion of fifteen more paces of the Wall, and he thought again of the men who had travelled the length of the Roman Empire to work and fight on these northern hills. Men of Tuscany and Syria, Egypt and North Africa. He inspected once more the Mithraic stone, symbol of the Roman army's personal god that had probably come from Brocolita, and he considered returning to add some shots to his collection but finally decided against the idea. He had enough material from Chesters; tomorrow he'd move on to the site at Housesteads where a replica of the Roman fort had been erected and where considerable archaeological investigation was still continuing. He would also take the opportunity to walk a section of the Wall itself and look out over the windswept hills where centuries ago, the barbarians had threatened the northern limits of the Roman empire.

Outside the museum the day was warm. The breeze had dropped and as he walked past the remains of the Roman commandant's house, the low wall of the barracks and the bath house, he traversed the ancient latrines and looked out across the slopes to the river. He reflected how all this peace would be far divorced from the ancient reality of the blood, the howl of the icy northern winds, the screaming of dark savages as they attempted to storm the milecastles that held them back from the rich lands to the south. He would write about such thoughts in his next book of illustrated essays.

Gilbert turned away and walked towards the car park. He carefully packed his photographic equipment into the boot of his four wheel drive – useful for investigating along the muddy tracks in the Cumbrian hills – and drove the short distance to The George Hotel at Chollerford. He hesitated, then thoughtfully unpacked all his gear and when the porter appeared, they together carried it all up to his room; he was a cautious man and the equipment had cost him a great deal of money.

After a shower he felt refreshed; he looked at himself in the mirror as he towelled himself down. He was still slim at forty, his fair hair was thinning a little at the crown but he was still presentable, he considered; clear eyes, good profile, only a hint of sagging at his jowls. Naked, he wandered out of the bathroom to the window and looked out over the terrace and the river bridge. He knotted the towel around his waist.

That was when he saw her.

She was standing in the gardens, quite alone, staring out towards the river bridge. She was tall, slimly built, long-legged, and she stood there with a casual, unaffected grace, one hand resting on the stone wall, almost as if she was posing for a portrait. Even from here he could see that her skin was tanned, her hair black, cut short to the graceful line of her neck. The thin red sweater she wore exposed her upper arms and was low cut to the swell of her bosom. He could not make out her features since she was half turned away from him, and she wore dark glasses, but he had no doubt that she was a beautiful woman.

Paul stood watching her for several minutes as his body dried under the towel. Unaware of his attention the woman stretched her arms, removed her sunglasses, looked up at the late afternoon sky, then strolled along the path out of his line of sight.

He sighed. After she had disappeared he regretted he had not had the presence of mind to reach for his camera, getting a shot not so much for his book but merely for his own pleasure. There had been something about her that had stirred him. He had not been in a relationship for some time now, travelling about the north as he had been, and the woman had a grace about her that reminded him of a panther, wild, free, untamed. He chewed at his lip, slightly annoyed with himself and then almost as though she had divined what he had in mind, she came back into his view. She had removed her dark glasses, and she held them in her left hand. As she paused again beside the stone bridge, above the gleam of the rushing river, Paul turned away, grabbed up his camera, clipped on the telephoto lens and waited until she paced a little nearer to his window.

He took several shots as she stood there; they would be good since almost unconsciously she moved like a professional model, seemed almost to take the kind of classical poses that magazine editors loved, but there was an underlining voluptu-ousness to her body that was unlike the cold distance affected by the women he had used as models in his earlier days.

He wondered what she would look like undressed.

She finally moved away from the bridge and he noted she

was taking the road towards the hotel. She moved out of his vision. He felt a vague excitement in his chest. He would be having dinner at the hotel. There was the chance she might be there ... possibly alone. Paul Gilbert walked to the small refrigerator in his room, took out a miniature bottle of whiskey and poured it into a glass. He cast aside the towel, sat in the easy chair and sipped at the drink, still thinking of the woman he had seen at the bridge. He observed his lower body with interest; the memory of her had an effect that did not surprise him. He had always been a sensual man.

When he had finished the whiskey he took another, then dressed carefully in a freshly laundered, open-necked shirt and light grey trousers. His skin tingled and he enjoyed a barely subdued feeling of expectation. He had the premonition that the remainder of his stay at Chollerford was going to be interesting.

Gilbert experienced a feeling of acute disappointment when the woman failed to appear in the dining room. The room was crowded; a large number of people had come out from Newcastle for some kind of celebration, and Gilbert was forced to relinquish the table he preferred, located near the window with a view over the gardens. His was a single table, near the door. It gave him a view of the whole room, and the noisy cele-bratory group ranged alongside the windows, but the woman he was looking for did not appear. He ate silently, accompanied his meal with a bottle of Pinot Grigio and tried to dampen down his frustration.

He was not disappointed later in the evening. After finishing his meal he decided to take a nightcap in the bar. He found a table in the corner, facing the door, and sat quietly, a little morose. While he sipped his drink, he observed the room but there was no one there who aroused his interest. He was still there when the bar gradually emptied and a small group of travellers – members of a cricket club it would seem from their rowdy conversation – finished their drinks and disappeared back to the car park; he heard the rumble of their car engines as they headed back towards Newcastle.

Eleven o'clock was chiming and he was about to relinquish his seat when the woman came in.

She looked at him; her glance held his for a few seconds. She had bright, sharp blue eyes, but there was something promisingly languorous in her glance as she seemed to look him up and down. It was not an indifferent inspection. Paul Gilbert felt a quickening of his pulse.

She moved towards the bar where the barman, who had earlier showed signs of hoping that his solitary customer would give up and go to bed, welcomed her with an ingratiating smile. Gilbert heard her ask for a whiskey straight. She eyed the clock and then suggested that the barman might wish to serve her in the residents' lounge. He nodded, she turned away, but as she left, she glanced briefly at Gilbert. Their eyes met and he watched her as she moved gracefully from the bar. There was little left in Gilbert's glass as, after a few minutes, he rose and followed her into the lounge.

His philosophy had always been that a man had to take his chances when they arose.

The woman was seated, one leg crossed elegantly over the other, on a settee near the window. Outside, the evening was darkening into the deep blue of northern summer evenings after the last distant, fading glow of the dying sun. He strolled towards her, then stood over her, smiling, with his half-empty glass in his hand.

'Bit late to start drinking,' he suggested.

She looked at him coolly, but made no reply. As he stood there, feeling slightly foolish, the barman came in with a tray and the whiskey. Just as he proffered it to the woman, Gilbert stepped forward.

'I'll take that. And could you bring me a brandy and soda?'

The barman glowered, hesitated then allowed Gilbert to take the bill from the tray. Gilbert glanced at it then said, 'You can add both drinks to my room number.'

The woman made no comment as he signed the bill with a flourish.

She took her drink from the tray while Gilbert stood above her and finished the half-empty glass in his hand. She stared at him with cool eyes as she sipped at the whiskey. But excitement coiled in Gilbert's veins as he realized she had raised no objection to his action.

He placed his empty glass on the table beside her. 'Didn't see you at dinner.'

She shrugged. 'I ate in my room. I like my own company.'

'It was a bit noisy. You were wise.'

She seemed distant yet she had accepted his paying for her drink, and there was something in her languorous attitude that made him feel his time would not be wasted.

'So,' he said slowly. 'I'm interested. Are you?'

He could read nothing in her eyes now, as she glanced at him. 'Interested? In what?' she asked after a few moments.

'In carrying on this conversation for a few hours.'

'I didn't think we were having a conversation.'

'It could develop into one. Or something else.'

Now, there was a hint of a smile upon her lips. They had a luscious curve to them. He felt he was making progress. He stared at her, suddenly grinning like an excited schoolboy. It seemed to him she was making up her mind about something, in a somewhat calculating fashion.

She showed her teeth in a smile: her teeth were white, even, and her smile seemed almost predatory. 'All right. I'm bored. I've nothing better to do, so, let's converse.'

'My name's Gilbert ... Paul Gilbert. I'm an author of sorts ... I produce photographic essays, and I'm doing one on Hadrian's Wall.'

'Photographic essays,' she considered soberly. 'I would have thought that's a bit old hat ... surely it's been done often before.'

Gilbert put her right on that score. He sat down beside her and enthusiastically, he told her of the crags above Whin Sill, the hills the centurions had watched, the savage raids of the men from the north; he tried to instil in her the excitement he felt at the exaltation of the romance and history of the Wall, and how he tried to capture that history and sensation in the photographs he composed. But after the barman had brought him his brandy he was disappointed to realize that he had not managed to stir her imagination, had made little impression upon her by his erudition, and had not succeeded in overcoming her languid, almost bored air. He was a little disappointed and more than a little desperate, he had hoped she would have possessed intellectual qualities as well as beauty. Although he admitted to himself it was not her mind he was really interested in, he would more than settle for a close physical relationship and he still felt it was more than a possibility.

When she had almost finished her drink he suggested they might take a walk on the terrace in the moonlight.

The moon was bright. It gleamed silver on the river. As they strolled, each with glass in hand, the woman's shoulder touched his briefly and he shivered.

'You haven't told me your name.'

She hesitated, as though considering that to give him her name would lead to an unwanted intimacy. Then she shrugged. 'Eileen,' she said at last and turned her face to his.

It was casual and yet meaningful. She raised her head slightly. It was with a certain surprise, mingled with excitement, that he leaned forward to kiss her. There was still a lingering disappointment in him when it was over. Her kiss had seemed very practised, almost professional but devoid of any emotion, and he felt it was as though she was merely experimenting, trying to determine whether she really wanted to be kissed. It was a curious experience, but on the other hand it was a start, and he was not the man to look a gift horse in the mouth, so to speak.

'How long are you staying at The George?' Gilbert enquired.

'Just tonight.'

'Then we don't have much time, do we?' he ventured.

'No. And it's beginning to get cold out here.'

This could be the start of something, he thought … or the end. He hoped it was the former. Certainly, there was something in her tone that suggested he should try his luck. So he asked, and she agreed almost immediately that they could share a drink from the mini-bar in her room, but that she'd like to go ahead.

Gilbert stood on the terrace after she had gone, alone in the gathering darkness, as he finished his drink.

It was all happening so quickly, and yet there was something cold and calculated in her attitude. Oddly enough that only served to increase his desire. His throat was dry. He had the impression she hardly saw him as a person, merely a man. He could have been anyone. A one night stand. Not that there was anything wrong with that. And though he liked directness he still felt in sexual matters there should be more … more of a civilized approach, a bantering, sexual innuendo, physical awareness, a savouring of the sexual opportunity. Like sipping good wine.

This had been too quick to be entirely satisfactory. But perhaps he was too much of a romantic. If she was available, why should he worry?

The thought of the woman's body still excited him. Ten minutes, she had suggested, but what was a matter of a few minutes between friends? He left the terrace, walked through the lounge and took the stairs to the first floor.

The corridor was quiet. She had told him she was in Room 14. When he reached her room he tapped lightly on the door with the tips of his fingers.

'Eileen?'

There was no immediate reply.

Gilbert waited, tapped again, more heavily this time but there was still no answer. The exulting smile began to harden on his mouth, and he chewed his lower lip. He knocked again but the silence grew around him as an angry knot began to form in his stomach. He tried the door, but it was firmly locked against him. A few minutes ago he had been feeling rather superior, aware of a vague disappointment that the woman hadn't played a long waiting game with him but prepared to accept all that she had to offer. Now that the feeling had evaporated, the ache in his loins had turned into a compound of desire and frustration and anger. He rapped his knuckles once more on the unresponsive door and then, as the fury of frustration began to mount in his chest he turned angrily away, marched down the corridor, went back to his own room.

She had made a fool of him, played with his feelings, probably had never had the intention of welcoming him into her room. He walked the length of his own bedroom, time and again, clenching his fists in the darkness. His skin felt sharply sensitive, his mouth was dry, and there was a pounding anger in his head. The flash of a car's headlights briefly illuminated the darkness of his room and he caught a glimpse of himself in the mirror. His eyes were bright with anger.

He undressed quickly, throwing his clothing savagely to the floor. He lay on his back in the bed, staring sleeplessly at the ceiling. He knew it was going to be a long, lonely night, scarred with his sexual frustration. He turned over, lay on his face, seeking to control the urgency of his body.

Gilbert's mood of black anger lasted through till dawn, outliving the frenzied twisting sleep that he tossed through. When he finally gave up, rose and went to the window he realized there had been a light rain during the night but the clouds had washed away under the morning sun. It was only six o'clock but Gilbert showered, dressed, walked out of the hotel and made his way along the road eastwards towards Chesters.

He did not want to face the woman's cool triumph at breakfast. She had led him on, played with him, made a fool of him and he would not allow her the satisfaction of seeing his sour countenance in the dining room. Even if she deigned to appear, though he suspected she might if only to enjoy his discomfiture. He took the footpath from Chollerford Bridge up to the abutment of the old Roman structure that had carried the walk and the Wall across the North Tyne. He stood and stared at the lewis holes that had been dug in the distant past, holes that had been used for lifting the great stone blocks of the Roman-built bridge, visible still after the centuries.

The phallus carved by a bored legionnaire centuries ago on one of the stones mocked him, sharpened the memory of his humiliation the previous evening.

Gilbert walked briskly back down to Chesters Fort, the wind cool on his burning face. He had an uninterrupted view of the river and all about him was quiet, the hills calm and green under the morning sun, a contrast with his raging fury. He cursed the woman. She had led him on and then she had lain in her bed, laughing into her pillow as he had knocked in frustration at her door. It would certainly not have been virginal fears that had made her bar the door to him; he remembered the confident expertise of her kiss.

He was unable to fathom why she had behaved the way she had, and the nagging ache was still in his body. He walked through the car park, paying little attention to the solitary car parked there. The gate to Chesters was open and he walked through, his hands in his pockets, shoulders hunched disconsolately.

The mood left Gilbert when he reached the ancient bath house. He stood on the remains of the Roman walls and once again looked down to what had been the hot bath house and the latrines, and he then turned away, walked towards the river, gazing over the slow-moving Tyne where it curved in a long, turgid bend at the bottom of the slope.

It was then that he saw the man's fingers.

They were curling lifelessly, half-closed. Against the rough hewn stone of the bath house wall, the dead thumb was cocked in a macabre gesture of male triumph.

CHAPTER TWO

IT WAS NOT the screaming from the next door apartment that offended Chief Inspector James Cardinal.

After all, in his view, the noise was connected to perfectly legitimate sexual activity on the part of the neighbours and was therefore none of his business. But his wife saw it in a different light. It was, she advised him, like living next door to a brothel. He was not sure how she felt able to make this comparison, having led as far as he was aware a somewhat sheltered life. And secretly he rather envied the vigorous activity that seemed to be going on next door; his own marriage held no such excitements. What offended him was his wife's insistence that he should do something about it.

She argued, 'What is the point in being a policeman if one couldn't sort such things out?' It was her constant complaint. It gave him a headache, one more fierce and less convenient than the one she regularly pleaded at weekends.

Partly as a consequence of the usual weekend nagging, when he entered the office on Monday morning he was in a bad temper, his brow furrowed with pain, unwilling as usual to seek relief in painkilling drugs, deeming it more appropriate to fight the pain by normal, natural means. The triumph of the will. His mood was not improved by the sight of Detective Sergeant Grout seated in Cardinal's chair in the office.

The sergeant rapidly leapt to his feet when Cardinal entered. Cardinal scowled; the sergeant clearly had ideas above his station. He grunted in dissatisfaction, aware that his mood was souring him. Maybe he was getting old. Maybe he ought to think about retiring. The prospect alarmed him. A lifetime of being nagged about unimportant, inconsequential matters. But was that being fair? They were important to his wife.

As for Sergeant Grout ... he was a good man, a solid, dependable officer occasionally endowed with flashes of flair and intelligence, the sort of man Cardinal needed at his side. Cardinal was aware that his own qualities depended upon a dogged persistence, rather than a sharp insight into the vagaries of human behaviour – he was a man who lived his professional life on a basis of stubbornness and hard work. Grout was different, he was able to supplement Cardinal's qualities by quite different abilities.

But there were occasions when Cardinal regretted that he had been forced to accept Grout into the detective squad based in York. He had been unable to resist the appointment, of course, the Chief Constable had spoken to him about it.

'The fact that young Grout is my nephew has nothing to do with the matter,' the Chief Constable had insisted. 'You can take a look at his file. The boy has qualities that we can use under your control. He's a bit headstrong, I admit, but you can knock that out of him. And from your point of view, James, you could perhaps profit from the assistance of a younger man ...' Here the Chief Constable had smiled like a predatory wolf. 'Someone not quite so dyed in the wool. You and I, we come from the old school, so Detective Sergeant Grout might bring some light into the darkened rooms of our experience....'

Darkened rooms, Cardinal thought grumpily. It was rumoured that the Chief Constable wrote poetry in his spare time. The fact was that Cardinal sometimes found Grout a bit too much to bear.

He hadn't really tried to work out why. Physically they were very different: Cardinal was tall, lean, narrow-featured; Grout was of a stocky peasant build, broad-shouldered with a disarmingly open visage. There was the fact that Grout was reading Law in his spare time – which Cardinal tried to keep to a minimum – and had acquired a working knowledge of Urdu, of all things, while James Cardinal thought only of putting his feet up during the rare occasions when he found himself not occupied in or pondering over the cases he was currently working on. But added to all this was the fact that Grout was of a personality that seemed difficult to ruffle. When Cardinal snarled at him Grout showed little reaction other than a setting of the lips and the raising of his chin a trifle. Even when Cardinal had caught him seated in the Chief Inspector's office, in Cardinal's own chair.

This irritated Cardinal, and left him with a vague feeling of inferiority, even if he was the senior officer.

Grout had scrambled out of the chair as Cardinal came in, but seemed unaffected by the scowl Cardinal had directed at him. The detective chief inspector now stood in front of the window, massaging his temple with probing fingers. Detective Sergeant Grout was in the office because Cardinal had summoned him, but the chief inspector was in no hurry to explain the reason, it would do Grout good to be kept waiting.

'Did you finish the report on the Elstrom manslaughter charge?' Cardinal asked at last, in a sour tone, as he stood staring sightlessly out of the window.

'It's on your desk, sir.'

'And the bribery offence?'

'It's with Maggie, being typed up. She reckons it'll be completed early this afternoon.'

Maggie. Cardinal flicked an angry glance over his shoulder. He did not approve of familiarity with the civilian staff. Grout seemed generally popular in headquarters and adapted socially with much more ease than Cardinal was capable of. He gritted his teeth, turned away from the window and sat in the chair behind his desk. Grout remained standing. Cardinal eyed him bleakly, making no secret of his mood.

'I believe you've put in for leave.'

'That's right, sir.'

'You're aware your work with the Squad must come first.'

'Of course, sir.'

'Time off will be difficult to organize,' Cardinal opined in a discontented mutter.

Grout nodded. 'I'm aware of the work load.'

Cardinal sighed heavily. 'Well, if I am to release you it will have to wait until we sort out this Clifford business.'

There was a short silence. 'Clifford?'

Cardinal was irrationally pleased at Grout's ignorance. The young man didn't have his ear to the ground at all times, clearly. Clifford's name was well-known in the squad room. The thought made Cardinal's mood lighten somewhat.

'Ah. So I haven't told you about Clifford, Sergeant. Someone the Chief Constable hasn't briefed you about.' The barb gave Cardinal a certain pleasure and he bared his teeth in a thoughtful grimace. 'Gus Clifford ... it's a sort of long-standing thing for me. You might hear, if you ask around the squad room, that it's developed into a sort of personal vendetta as far as I'm concerned. If there's one man in the world I'd like to see slammed into a cell it's that bastard Clifford.'

27

'I've not heard of him, sir.' Grout said, a little stiffly.

'No.'

Cardinal was silent for a little while, frowning. He wished this bloody headache would subside. Thoughts of Clifford only made it worse. He stared at his slim, elegant hands placed on the desk in front of him. An artist's hands, his wife had once told him, many years ago. The Clifford thing went back a long way, almost as long as that comment, back to Cardinal's early days as an inspector, before he had moved north for promotion to the York office. His wife had never really liked the Met anyway. Too many villains, she reckoned, and she rarely got to see him, even at weekends. Not that life had changed much for her in York.

But Cardinal would be the first to admit that Clifford had become almost an obsession with him.

In a sense his attitude demonstrated Clifford's efficiency and cunning; while the man's evasiveness was partly due to the restrictions that hampered police work, he was also a remarkably slippery customer. On three occasions Gus Clifford had been hauled in on serious charges, only to escape scot-free when witnesses disappeared, or changed their testimony … and once on a legal technicality concerning which Cardinal had been hauled over the coals for letting dislike blind his judgement. He remembered the last time he had seen Clifford. Big, hulking shoulders, a sneering confidence on his mouth, eyes that expressed contempt for the man who was facing him.

'He's been leading a charmed life, has Clifford,' Cardinal acknowledged bitterly, 'but one of these days I'll pin his ears back for good.'

'He's operating here in the north, sir?'

Cardinal swivelled in his chair so he could see the map of northern England pinned to the wall. His domain, his manor, the area covered by the detective squad he led, was delineated in red. He nodded towards the map. 'You see that, Grout? It's our patch. But now Gus Clifford has edged his way into our jurisdiction. I wouldn't be surprised if Clifford's got one just like it in his office, wherever his bloody office is. He's no fool and he's a good organizer.'

'I don't understand, sir.'

Cardinal grimaced sourly. 'He first came to my notice when I was with the Metropolitan Police. He was involved in the protection rackets in those days, but we had problems pinning him down even then. He never saw himself as small time in his activities; it wasn't long before he began to expand, and moved into prostitution. He set up deals with traffickers in Eastern Europe and even South East Asia, and the Philippines. He had a hand in organizing brothels in the less salubrious areas of the Smoke. But we could never pin him down, he always seemed to be able to keep people quiet by the simple expedient of threats of violence. Along with the occasional torching of premises. Anyway, by the time we finally managed to crack down on that business, with a certain success, he had moved on and he opened up other sidelines, like smuggling cigarettes on an industrial scale, though his main business soon became the distribution of drugs. We tried to put him inside for the establishment of bogus companies and fraud scams but he could afford a smart Queen's Counsel who made a fool of us and our efforts. We were left with egg on our faces, and he was there laughing at us.'

Cardinal glowered at the map, massaged his temples again, almost unconsciously as the pent up anger in his chest began to get the better of him.

'Since then, things have moved on. I came up here, and Clifford, well, he seems to have got involved in more sophisticated – and maybe less openly brutal – forms of crime. He's moved into a new racket, I'm informed. You know much about the art world, Grout?'

'I know a Constable from a Sargent, sir.'

Cardinal turned his chair slowly around to glare at the detective sergeant. 'I can do without the laboured humour, Grout.' He grimaced, then sighed despondently. 'Clifford moved into the art world some years ago in style. The information I've received suggests he's been involved in the organization of most of the art thefts in the country houses on the fringe of the London area over the last five years. But apart from paintings he's also moved into a lucrative system of scams involving antiques. There's a packet to be made from the States and Europe. I'm told the big museums aren't too careful about demanding appropriate provenance for the items they've offered. A lot of the stuff is looted from designated – and protected – sites scattered throughout Europe and in particular, Italy. I'm informed there are always unscrupulous curators who are always keener to add to their collections in their museums, publicly endowed as well as private. Yes, it seems they're prepared to accept the doubtful if not fake details that Clifford and his associates, his front men, are able to provide. Clifford has built up a network throughout Europe, and has been selling to the States, China, Switzerland – where he's got a warehouse hidden away somewhere, but he's now carved up the whole of England into organized areas.'

'I … I'm not certain what you mean. Areas for what purpose?' Grout asked, still puzzled.

'He's got ten territories, each with a nominated agent at its head, responsible to him. There's the south west, the south, the metropolitan, the south east to cover that part of the country. Farther north he's got a midland area organized from

Birmingham, a north western based in Liverpool, a Yorkshire, northern and Scottish series of operations.'

'This sounds the stuff of fantasy, sir. Are you sure of this? We've all heard of a fabulous Mr Big in criminal fraternities but this …' He wrinkled his nose. 'You said ten territories, sir.'

'We mustn't forget Wales, Grout,' Cardinal said dryly. 'Never forget Wales. If you spoke Welsh instead of bloody Urdu I'd be inclined to send you down there to check on what I'm telling you. But forget Mr Big. Clifford is just a small-time crook who's made it by extending his activities with existing networks throughout Europe. He's just one of many. But the others, they don't concern me. Gus Clifford is big enough for me. I want … I *have* to nail that bastard!'

Grout hesitated. 'How exactly are you involved in all this, sir?'

'The fact of the matter,' Cardinal said, 'is that when I was with the Met I was the officer in charge when we finally pulled in Clifford. I got to know him well. We had some interesting conversations, on and off the record, before his smart-arse lawyer got him off all charges. He walked free, and I was embarrassed and furious. And I came north. But somehow it felt like a defeat.' Cardinal scratched thoughtfully at his cheek. 'But things come around, don't they? It seems as though others have come to realize that Clifford needs stopping. New information recently came in – the other regions have come to understand what's going on, the network is now an established fact and we've been drawn into an investigation that spans the regions. And we are closely involved because of my knowledge of the bastard. I've been asked to co-ordinate the hunt from here in York. I'm telling you all this, Grout, to explain why I won't be around much to keep an eye on you during the coming weeks.'

Grout frowned. 'I don't need nursing, sir.'

'Debateable. And I do sometimes wonder who's running this bloody office,' Cardinal said.

Grout stiffened but made no response.

'*Maggie*,' Cardinal growled in contempt. When Grout showed no reaction, he went on. 'Anyway, I was down in London on Friday at a conference of the senior officers from the Met, and in particular people from Northumberland and Cumbria. Clifford has been very active in the north and has finally overextended himself. It looks as though we've struck lucky at last. A certain disaffected gentleman has seen fit to rat on Gus Clifford – faced as he is with a lengthy term inside for fraud – and we are told there is shortly to be a meeting of the Board.'

'Board? I don't understand, sir,' Grout murmured.

'They now seem to regard themselves as businessmen, these criminal scumbags. Clifford has what he calls a Board … the individual heads of his network, his areas, and they are to meet in London tomorrow. We're lined up to pounce on them. Not only will they all be conveniently gathered in one place, but there should be enough in their individual briefcases to put them all away for a number of years. Even so, once we get them in the net there's going to be a lot of hard digging to do in the next few weeks to sort things out so it's unlikely you'll be getting Inspector rank until I get back. The paperwork, you know. And as for leave … well, you see how it is.'

'*Inspector*?' Grout had not been aware he was in line for promotion. He opened his mouth in surprise but Cardinal cut him off coldly before he could speak.

'Friends in high places, hey? Don't let it get to your head, Grout.' He got up, walked across to the map on the wall, prodded at it with his lean finger, traced the line along the

Yorkshire border. 'Inspector Elliott will be going down to London this afternoon and I'll be awaiting confirmation from him that Clifford's northern agent will have boarded the train. We've been tagging him for some time; he never flies down because apparently our bold criminal isn't happy about taking to the air. Takes all sorts.... The rest of the mob will be converging for the meeting this afternoon and tonight. We know the location: a small hotel in Russell Square. Nothing fancy. Clifford believes in keeping a low profile. So, we have the troops on standby. Tomorrow we'll catch the lot of them, bag them like rats in a trap. Along with the big cheese himself.' Cardinal rolled the name around his tongue with obvious satisfaction. 'Big Gus Clifford.'

As Grout stood there in front of him, Cardinal seemed suddenly to become aware of the gloating tone in his voice. He grimaced, and returned abruptly to his desk to sit down once more. 'All right, enough of all that. I called you in here to explain to you how it is, how it's going to be. I won't be around much over the next few weeks. I'll be pretty busy with the Clifford business. That means you'll need to pick up the overview on the Endbury and Cooper cases from Inspector Maxwell. He'll be taking over some of my duties, acting as my deputy, and won't have time for—'

Cardinal was interrupted by a knock on the door. He raised his head and called out. The door opened and a fresh-faced young constable from the outer office entered the room.

'This had better be important,' Cardinal snarled.

The young constable licked his lips nervously, glanced at Grout. Cardinal could guess what the young man would be saying when he got back with his colleagues: *His Eminence the Cardinal is in a right mood today.*

'This message has just come in from Chief Superintendent

Carliss, sir. I thought you'd want to see it immediately.'
Cardinal took the proffered paper and read it quickly. His lean
features took on a grimmer aspect. His lips writhed back as
he gestured to the constable to leave, and while Grout waited
patiently Cardinal picked up the phone and dialled a London
number. He waited, tapping his fingers impatiently on the
desk.

'Bill? Cardinal here. I've just got the message. What the hell's
going on?' His tone was impatient.

Grout waited and watched as Cardinal's mouth drooped in
ill-disguised disappointment. The chief inspector said nothing
more during the next two minutes as the man at the other end
of the phone continued. When Cardinal did finally speak, he
was terse. 'I see. That puts us back where we started. Right. I'll
see what I can do this end to try to pull them in.'

He banged down the receiver in obvious anger. He glared at
Grout, as though blaming him for what had happened. 'Bloody
meeting's cancelled.'

'Clifford's meeting, you mean?'

'What other meeting would I be talking about?' Cardinal
said savagely. 'The meeting of the bloody Board's been
cancelled and as far as I can gather our informant, our inside
man, is reckoning that all the area heads have been ordered to
go to ground. Wherever they can find a personal rat hole.'

Grout hesitated. 'They got scared? So what happens now?'

'Clearly they got wind of our operation. How the hell...?
Anyway, we'll now have to scrabble around the regions to pull
in the bastards one by one,' Cardinal said with an angry snap
to his tone. 'And that means a lot of extra bloody hard work
and trouble that we didn't need at this stage. I didn't want this
complication, believe me. I thought it was all sewn up at last.
Now we'll have to charge ahead but without all the evidence

we need. In some cases, my guess is all we can do is give them scare, alert them, maybe fix them with receiving if we can find their local warehouses, but the whole damn thing is a mess, Grout, a real mess.' Cardinal rose abruptly, marched to the door, flung it open and bawled, 'Where the hell's Robinson? Why hasn't he reported in yet?'

Hastily, Grout pushed past the senior officer and stepped into the corridor. 'I'll check at once, sir, and get a call out to the patrol car.'

'Do that. Contact Inspector Parker at Leeds while you're at it. Fill him in, ask for his co-operation and he'll know what you mean when you say that Elliott needs to get hold of the guy he's been observing. He needs to be arrested, brought in for questioning.'

'Elliott has been observing...?'

'He's been keeping an eye on our weak link in Clifford's organization! A man who apparently has ideas above his station. He's called Rigby – and he was scheduled to go down for the Board meeting. I thought I already told you that! Keep up, Grout, keep up, for God's sake!'

As Grout made his way, stiff-lipped, to the outer office, Cardinal walked back into his room and banged the door behind him. He stood by the window, gradually cooling down, suppressing the painful ache of anger in his chest. The way things were going on he'd probably end up with a heart attack. Clifford, the enthusiastically copulating neighbours, his wife's constant complaints ...

He stared out across the sunlit roofs to the ancient cathedral where the tourists would be thronging, through the Shambles, walking along the city walls, past Clifford's Tower, dining down by the river. He wondered briefly whether his old enemy Gus Clifford might have been distantly related to the Norman robber baron who had built the tower. The follower of Duke William the Conqueror would no doubt have been as violent and unprincipled as the man who had been getting under Cardinal's skin for years.

Several minutes passed before the telephone on Cardinal's desk rang. He picked up the receiver. 'Robinson?'

Robinson's voice was partly masked by the sound of traffic roaring in the background. 'Yes, sir. Sorry I've not called in earlier but I've just spoken to Inspector Elliott. He's been hanging around waiting to see if Rigby boarded the next train out of Newcastle.'

'He wasn't on the first?' Cardinal asked, glancing at his watch.

'No, sir. Anything gone wrong?'

'You could bloody well say so. The meeting's been cancelled. That's why your looking out for Rigby is useless, he won't be heading south. He'll be off to the woods somewhere.'

'So what now, sir?'

'Put the call out. Pick him up if you can. You've got some men on standby, and someone on surveillance at his home. Get there straight away. I'll send a couple of squad cars as back-up but you'd better liaise as of right with the Newcastle and Northumberland police at Ponteland, keep them in the picture. For God's sake, let's have no slip-ups. I want you to bring Rigby here to me at York, alive and kicking, along with Inspector Elliott. Rigby, alive, kicking, and I hope squealing his ugly head off!'

'I'll get things moving straight away, sir.'

Robinson rang off.

Cardinal replaced the receiver, stared at it for several seconds then looked up as Detective Sergeant Grout tapped on the door and entered. Cardinal didn't like what he saw.

The normally expressionless sergeant was frowning and his thick lips were set. Cardinal had rarely seen that expression. It meant inevitably there was a problem.

'Tell me,' Cardinal said, suddenly even more wearily despondent.

'You've spoken to Robinson?'

'I have. Rigby didn't turn up to take the train to London for the Board meeting.'

Grout nodded as though he already knew. He had a slip of paper in his hand, a message from the operations room.

'This came in earlier, sir. It wasn't drawn to our attention because the duty sergeant didn't realize its significance and thought Inspector Maxwell should be the man to deal with it but—'

'Spit it out, Grout!'

'Robinson won't have any difficulty finding Rigby, whom I gather is one of Clifford's associates.'

'And the only man we can pin down up here! That's why we've had him under observation, for God's sake. He's been our link to Clifford. But he won't be difficult to find? How do you work that out?'

'The body of a man was discovered early this morning at Chesters Fort in Northumberland. The back of his head was battered in. He's very dead, sir. As a doornail, one might say.'

Cardinal sighed. There was something quite old-fashioned about Detective Sergeant Grout.

Dead as a doornail. 'So?'

'The dead man has been identified, sir. His name is Joseph Frederick Rigby.'

Detective Chief Inspector Cardinal could not suppress a groan. Their link to Gus Clifford was gone.

CHAPTER THREE

GROUT GUESSED THAT there would be a certain amount of pressure on the parking space at Chesters so he left his car at The George Hotel car park and walked the short distance past the stone bridge towards the ancient Roman camp. The narrow road that swung up the hill to his right was part of the old Roman military way that sliced through the hard quartz dolerite hills towards Carlisle. He thought he would like to tramp that road at some time … but when would there be time? Chesters Fort lay beyond the narrow belt of trees ahead of him.

The parking area beyond the first gate was guarded by two uniformed policemen and the entrance was taped off. Some disconsolate gentlemen of the Press were standing by, clearly niggled by the fact they were denied entrance, and by the paucity of information that had so far been provided to them. Grout made his way past them, only one of them half-heartedly raising a hand and asking a question but Grout ignored him, presented his identity card to the officers, and was allowed to step inside the perimeter sealed off with tape.

He made his way towards the cluster of officers huddled near the entrance to Chesters Museum and introduced himself.

The man in charge, a burly, chubby-featured police inspector looked him up and down. 'Grout. You'll be working with Cardinal, down at York HQ, you say.' The man's eyes had narrowed suspiciously, squinting against the brightness of the sun. 'So what's your interest in this business? This is all a bit away from your normal stamping ground.'

'The dead man is called Rigby.'

'We know that.'

'We were going to pull him in today.'

The police inspector raised interested eyebrows. 'Why?'

'We were hoping to get some information from him. An on-going investigation,' Grout replied reluctantly.

'You don't say. Well, you're a bit late, Sergeant. He won't be telling you much now.' The inspector writhed back his lips in a grimace. 'Not with the back of his head bashed in.'

Grout recognized the truculence in the man's tone; he was aware of it and to some extent had expected it. In the past he had felt the same way himself, in Leeds, before he had joined DCI Cardinal at York. It was always a matter of manors, of responsibilities, of stamping grounds, of turf wars. He waited, until the uniformed officer spoke again.

'I'm Inspector Waters. We'll be running the investigation into this killing. You may have been trying to haul this guy in, but he's gasped his last on our patch. So the rest now is up to us. Just what exactly do *you* hope to achieve around here?'

Grout shrugged. His tone was neutral, careful. 'DCI Cardinal would like to know the circumstances surrounding the man's death. As I said, Rigby was due to be pulled in for questioning with regard to a national inquiry that's been under way. It may be there's something significant our own investigations will turn up. Apart from what you find, I mean. We'd appreciate your co-operation.'

'And you'll get it,' Inspector Waters murmured with an underlying lack of conviction in his tone. He paused, reflecting. 'Rigby... He's known to us, of course. Petty villainy, bit of a record, and he'll be no loss to the community. Our guess is he's been clobbered in some gang quarrel or other.... We better get something straight, though, Grout. You got no real standing here, right?'

'I'm aware of that, Inspector.'

Waters was little mollified by the quick assurance offered. 'This will be a locally controlled investigation ... until I hear otherwise from the Chief Constable at Ponteland. I'm not interested in what the York office have got on Rigby unless it can bring a quick end to our own enquiries.

'Your investigations are national, you say? Well, I've heard nothing about that and I've got a dead man on my hands. So this is my responsibility. Now, I've no objection to your keeping a watching brief on all this, provided you don't get in my way, but I want you to be clear about this: I won't accept interference. This is our operation. Beyond that,' he waved his hand in a magnanimous gesture, 'help yourself. Don't get too close to the crime scene, of course, forensics haven't finished yet. In short, don't get in the bloody way. Otherwise ...'

He was about to turn away when Grout asked, 'Where was the body found?'

'Down there, near the bath house. Here ...' He called to a young constable standing nearby. 'Stocks, this is DS Grout. Up from the delights of the fleshpots of York. Stocks will show you the location, answer any questions you got, and keep you out of mischief. That all right, Stocks? OK. But before you leave the site, DS Grout, perhaps you'll have another word with me. So you can sort of fill me in about what exactly may be DCI Cardinal's interest in our corpse. In a spirit of mutual co-operation, if you know what I mean. That sort of thing. I'll probably be inside the museum.'

Inspector Waters turned away. Constable Stocks nodded affably to Grout and led the way towards the low walls of the bath house, Roman ruins that had been excavated many years ago. They tramped across the sward, avoiding the dusty churned ruts that had baked hard in the sun and wind, skirted the remains of what had been the Roman commandant's house and crossed the trimmed grass where a screen had been erected. It covered the lower part of the Roman structure that had served as a bath house and latrines. Under cover Grout saw three white-coated technicians at work, with a sports-jacketed civilian overseeing the operation. Grout guessed he'd be the forensic scientist brought in from the forensic laboratory at Gosforth.

'I think they'll be carting the body off pretty soon,' Stocks murmured. 'Looks like they've all but finished. Senior patholo-gist, he's been and gone already. They're just tidying up now, I think.' There was a certain casual self-importance in the constable's tone, an attempt to leave the impression that this was all in a day's work for him. Grout doubted that. It was likely this was Stocks's first murder case. But the constable would never admit that to an outsider.

The plastic shell was waiting for its burden. Grout stepped into the tent. The body had now been moved from the spot where it had been discovered but that didn't concern him much. The photographers would have done their job and no doubt he'd be given access to their work in due course. But he was curious to get a glimpse of the man called Rigby. He stepped forward to the plastic shell where the body was being lowered inside its cover.

'Can I take a look at him?' Grout asked.

One of the technicians glanced at Constable Stocks, who nodded. The technician unzipped the corpse. Grout leaned forward, the features were fixed and waxen now but he guessed the dead man would have been in his mid-thirties when his life was brought to an abrupt and violent end. About five feet nine, he calculated, hair thinning in the front, cheek-bones that now seemed to jut through skin that had become almost transparent in death.

'Back of his head was crushed in,' Constable Stocks said conversationally. 'Wouldn't be surprised that he had it coming to him. Like Inspector Waters said, he's known to us. I believe he's got a record, but nothing of recent years. Started as a kid, I believe, twocking cars down in the west end of Newcastle. From that he moved on to a bit of drug dealing in South Shields too, I believe. Stuff coming in from the boats docking at Jarrow. We keep an eye on the Slake, along with the Durham Police, sort of joint operation, but those operations have died down a bit recently as far as I can gather. So we haven't seen too much of friend Rigby recently. Been quiet, like. Moved into other stuff I don't doubt.' Stocks scratched at his ear, reflectively. 'There's been talk he might have had a hand in other scummy stuff. Like the East European girl trade and that sort of thing. That's the chat. Romanian whores. A few Poles. I always think they're handsome women, those Romanian and Poles. Anyway—'

'Was there anything of significance found on the body?' Grout interrupted.

Constable Stocks shrugged. 'Dunno about that, I've just been on duty up here an hour or so, but Inspector Waters will be able to fill you in on all that sort of thing. But the chatter is that from what we can make out it looks as though he wasn't actually killed here. He got his head bashed in somewhere up near the museum. He was dragged down here afterwards. To hide the body I suppose, chance to gain a few hours, I expect.'

'So who found him?'

Constable Stocks screwed up his eyes, wrinkled his nose. 'Ah, it was some guy called Gilbert, I believe. Photographer, apparently. He'd been staying at the hotel down by the bridge, The George at Chollerford. His story is he was out for a stroll in the early morning. Our lads have been questioning him down at The George this morning. He may well have been taken into Newcastle by now.'

Grout nodded thoughtfully. 'Have forensics come up with a likely time of death?'

'Like always,' the young constable announced importantly, as though he were an expert in such matters, 'they wouldn't say straight off but the lads tell me they did give a rough sort of estimate. They think he was hammered some time about midnight or maybe early hours of this morning.'

'And he was killed up there, near the museum,' Grout murmured, looking back to the entrance where he had briefly met Inspector Waters.

'Yeah, that's right. And there's another thing. You won't know, of course, but the museum got broken into last night. Could have been Rigby, I suppose, but on the other hand it could have been the man who clobbered him. Thieves falling out, that sort of thing.'

An unlikely scenario, Grout felt. 'So was anything taken from the museum?' he asked.

'Don't know about that. Can't say. They're still checking that out as far as I know. You talk to Inspector Waters, he'll be the one who can fill you in.' The constable had reddened somewhat; perhaps he suddenly felt he had been talking too much to an officer he did not know, and one from outside the force.

'Yeah. Maybe I'd better do that. Thanks anyway.'

Grout took another walk around the bath house as a matter of interest, historical rather than police procedural, for he knew full well it was highly unlikely he would find anything the locals or the forensic team would have missed. Then he made his way back across the field towards the museum.

The uniformed policeman at the entrance looked bored, standing to one side of the door in the shade. He told Grout that the inspector was to be found in the storeroom so Grout entered the building and wandered through the rooms, glancing at some of the exhibits, seeing nothing exceptionally interesting. He knew there was a more extensive museum now located at Housesteads, complete with facsimile copies of the letters written by the wife of the Roman commandant two thousand years ago, inviting friends to dinner, listing items to be bought for meals, trivia that were fascinating to the modern mind, showing that nothing really had changed in society over the centuries. He moved towards the steps leading down to the storeroom.

Inspector Waters was standing at the foot of the steps, just inside the doorway, talking to a man Grout assumed was the curator. He glanced up, saw Grout, then ignored his presence. There was dust in the air; the smell of inadequate ventilation touched Grout's nostrils.

Grout stood in the doorway, looking over the inspector's shoulder. Upstairs the exhibits had been carefully arranged, ticketed, described, but down here the items stored had been placed on shelves without description. He noted a few pieces of statuary in poor condition and it was clear that English Heritage had clearly placed upstairs most figurines they regarded of interest to the general public, or had moved them to the more tourist-orientated museum at Housesteads, some miles away, where excavations were still continuing and the replica milecastle had been built.

Grout was aware that over the centuries, much of the stone of Hadrian's Wall had suffered from the depredations of farmers and sheepherders who had used Roman-cut stone to build their walls and shelters over the years.

Inspector Waters turned to glance at Grout. 'You had a good look around then?'

'Yes, thank you,' Grout replied quietly. 'Constable Stocks was most helpful. But I understand there was a break in here as well ... as well as the killing up above.'

The curator muttered indignantly. He was an elderly, balding, small man with a narrow, wind-lined face and tired eyes. Grout guessed he would have been working here for many years, and would not be far off retirement; this was probably the first time events of such a catastrophic nature would have occurred on his watch. He was clearly as upset by the desecration of his kingdom as by the fact of a death at the site.

'Disgraceful,' he muttered. 'Quite disgraceful.'

'Has anything of value been taken?' Grout asked as Inspector Waters, cold-eyed, stood aside.

'*Everything* here is of value,' the curator snapped in irritation.

'Yes, but—'

'Can't understand,' the uniformed inspector intervened, 'can't understand why anyone would want to break in here. Value, you say?' he challenged the curator. 'In my view there's nothing of real value except maybe to students of history and tourists. Bits of old stone from the Wall. The odd carving with Roman numerals and names. Anyway, as far as we can see nothing's been taken from down here. Is that not right?' he challenged the curator again.

'Nothing taken? That's not the point!' the curator observed angrily, rubbing his hand over his bald head in frustration at the policeman's attitude. 'The fact there's been a break in at the museum, that's enough! As for anything being taken, you're a bit premature, Inspector Waters. I haven't really had time to make an absolutely detailed check.'

'You told me—'

'I said it doesn't look as though any of the exhibits up above have been touched,' the curator muttered defensively.

'What about down here?' Grout asked, after a short silence.

The little man shook his head, rubbed a doubtful finger against his nose and looked back behind him. He heaved a disconsolate sigh. 'There's been some disturbance here, but nothing seems to be missing. You must realize all items of real significance, material the public would be interested in seeing, or for research, are kept up above. Down here in the storeroom we have items that are still open to study, or which can be used by students from university archaeological departments as examples … like that Mithraic stone over there. I remember the day when they found the Mithraic temple on the Wall. Before that everyone thought he was just a minor deity of Persian origin, but once the temple was unearthed it soon became clear that Mithras was a powerful god, the favourite deity of the Roman army, a god who—'

'Yes, yes,' Waters intervened brusquely. It was clear to Grout that the inspector had already been subjected to a barrage of unwanted historical information by the little curator. 'That'll do for now, at any rate. The thing is, to assist in our investigation you'll need to carry out a thorough check both upstairs and down here. That way we can be certain that nothing really has been taken. The sooner you can let us have a definitive statement, the better. It may well be the break in is linked to the murder, but on the other hand it might have been someone other than the killer, or even Rigby himself, who was messing about here. In which case, who knows? Maybe we have a witness to what went on up above.' Softening somewhat at the pained expression on the curator's lined features, he patted the little man on the shoulder. 'Anything you can come up with, let us know. It could be important.'

The curator nodded unhappily, then led the way back up the stairs after closing the storeroom door. It was left unlocked, Grout noted. At the top of the stairs, Inspector Waters watched the curator amble off with slumped, disappointed shoulders to his office, presumably to retrieve the books in which records of the holdings would be kept. He sighed, gazed around him. The tiny dust motes drifted about them, dancing and flickering in the sunlight that came in through the high window.

Waters shook his head. 'Beats me why anyone would want to break in here and lump out any of this lot. Could have been kids, of course, just out to vandalize the place. Maybe they were disturbed by what went on with Rigby, and scarpered back to wherever they came from. Chances of finding them are remote, is my guess. Young layabouts from Chester-le-Street, or the west end of Newcastle....'

'It would surely be a long way for them to come, to break in here,' Grout pondered. 'And I can't imagine what they might have been hoping to find. What could they possibly be after?'

'Entrance money? I got no idea. Who knows what goes through the heads of kids these days?'

Grout looked about him uncertainly. 'You've thought of the possibility that it was Rigby himself who broke in?'

Inspector Waters stared at Grout for a few moments, then shrugged doubtfully. 'Maybe. But I can't see it would be his style. The forensic boys may come up with something to support that idea. I mean, what the hell would a villain like Rigby expect to find in this Godforsaken place?'

Carefully, Grout suggested, 'My information is that he's been involved recently in some dicey dealings involving works of art.'

Waters stared at him. 'I see. That's why Cardinal is interested in Rigby, hey? Art thefts. But there's no bloody Picassos or da Vincis here, believe me. Nothing I can see here which would be tempting to an art thief. It's just lumps of stone and bits of tiles. Still … you had a brief look around the site. While you were wandering around with Stocks, did your own perfectly trained investigative eye,' he added sarcastically, 'pick up anything us local yokels might have missed?'

Grout shook his head. 'I just wanted to check out the location. I'm sure your team will have done all that's necessary.'

'Pleased to have your approbation,' Waters grunted unenthusiastically. 'Anyway, I'm through here for the time being. I'm off back down to The George Hotel. We've been taking statements from some of the staff down there, to find out what they were all up to around the time we think Rigby was killed. I'd better see how things are going.'

'Would it be OK if I come along?' Grout asked tentatively.

The police inspector hesitated, grimaced. 'I'm not sure it'll do you any good. You'll have access to our report, I guess, in due course. Once the release has been cleared back in Ponteland. Thing is, you'll just be under our feet, you know what I mean? But I'll check it out. Now I need to get on.'

Grout was not surprised by the man's attitude. There was always local resistance to outside interference. Or even assistance. As Inspector Waters ambled out of the museum to make his way back to his car, Grout wandered in the direction taken by the curator. He found him seated in his office, poring over some heavy ledgers and a catalogue. He glanced up at Grout, then sighed and for the moment chose to ignore his presence. He rose, clutching the catalogue and went back to the exhibit room, checking off the items, clucking his tongue quietly as he did so. Grout leaned against the wall with folded arms, watched him for a while. He could understand the doubts in Inspector Waters's mind, there could hardly be anything here that would attract a thief of Rigby's inclination … or even young thugs from the west end for that matter. But what was Rigby doing out here at Chesters anyway? He was supposed to be making his way to London for Gus Clifford's Board meeting, according to DCI Cardinal.

'You have all this material up here catalogued, I see,' Grout called out to the curator, 'but what of the stuff in the storeroom below? Do you have a list of all the items there?'

The curator jerked his narrow head in surprise as though he had forgotten Grout's presence. He frowned.

'No catalogue, no. No printed record for public consumption, like up here. But it's not unimportant material we keep down in the storeroom. It all has its interest, its importance. It's merely that down there we keep articles that are of more interest to specialists, for study, rather than exhibition. We have regular visitors from the universities of Newcastle, Northumbria, and Durham, mainly the archaeological departments. Several of the professors use material held by us as a teaching resource. They've borrowed items from time to time, they arrange visits here for some of the students as well as encourage them to do work on the dig still going on up at Housesteads and elsewhere on the Wall. So they'll have a pretty good idea of what's down there, especially Professor Godfrey. Since he's been in charge of the Newcastle University Antiquities section, he's been here regularly. He's made extensive use of our facilities of recent years.'

'Professor Godfrey?'

'Yes, you must have heard of him,' the curator said impatiently. 'He's recognized as an authority on Roman antiquities, oh, yes, indeed. He wrote a monograph on the Wall a few years back ... we have a copy up in the exhibition, in fact, most instructive, most instructive. The Wall and the milecastles and Mithraic influences... He's encouraged his students to use our facilities a great deal. It was his antiquities section that sponsored the survey that was done here last year....' He paused as though irritated that he was being kept from his duties by Grout's questioning. 'As I told you, sorry, there's no catalogue as such regarding the materials and artefacts that are held here in the storeroom. But I'm sure Professor Godfrey can assist you if you wanted to find out what importance our holdings might be to historical research.'

Grout could tell the curator was not only irritated by Grout's presence, he seemed a little embarrassed that there seemed to be a flaw in the records and security procedures used at the museum. There seemed little point in flustering him further. He nodded, and walked away, back into the sunlight.

He was surprised to see that Inspector Waters was still there, getting out of his car. The officer waved his mobile at Grout. He seemed irritated.

'Just been in touch with HQ. Had a call. It seems your superior – DCI Cardinal himself – has just cleared lines with the Chief Constable. We are now supposed to offer you freedom of the manor, so to speak. You can come along to The George, stand by if you like while we're taking statements.' He glared at Grout, making little attempt to hide the animosity in his eyes. 'But let's be clear about one thing. Whatever your boss, and for that matter whatever the Chief Constable says, you've still got no standing in this business as far as I'm concerned. We run the operational unit, this is our scene of crime, and while you can listen in, I don't want you under our feet. *Capisce*?'

It was probably the only Italian Inspector Waters knew. It would have been gleaned from films such as *The Godfather*.

Grout nodded. He smiled slightly as the inspector turned back to his car. Even the engine roaring into life seemed to throw out a measure of defiance to the powers that be Detective Chief Inspector Cardinal of the York office, or Chief Constable of the Northumbrian police. As the door of Waters's car slammed and the driver pulled away from the car park, Grout smiled. He was not being offered a lift. But it was no great distance to The George Hotel at Chollerford. A pleasant walk in the sunshine, nothing more.

The hotel manager at The George Hotel had set aside a conference room on the first floor where the police could interview witnesses. Grout managed to insert himself into the room, standing quietly at the back while statements were being taken and witnesses interviewed. The constable on duty outside in the corridor had asked to see his ID but had clearly been forewarned of the likelihood that Grout would turn up. He entered as the barman was making a statement, and he remained as a group of other staff, including waitresses and room cleaners were put through their paces. It all became a matter of routine, drudgery even, and Grout became bored. None of the people interviewed seemed to have seen Rigby, or noted anything of significance and Grout began to feel he might have been better employed back at Chesters, with the remainder of the forensic team who were still searching the locality in the hope of finding the murder weapon.

It was only when the hotel night porter was interviewed,

however, that his interest quickened.

The porter was about sixty years of age, slightly bowed, but elegant in his immaculate if somewhat faded uniform. His grey, thinning hair was swept back neatly, his moustache was carefully trimmed and he showed himself in no way overawed by the situation. He exhibited a certain stubborn pride, in his appearance, his position and his responsibilities.

'Now let's get this straight,' Inspector Waters was saying. 'You were on duty from six in the evening until six next morning?'

'That's right, Inspector. My normal hours. Of course, I'd be dozing in my cubbyhole for a considerable part of that time, because well, there's nothing much happening if you know what I mean, once any latecomers have gone off to their beds. Dead of night, there's rarely even a mouse stirring. I check the keys rack, of course, to make sure no one is locked out, and then I settle down with my evening paper, but after that I have a snooze. Put my feet up. Until dawn. The manager knows about that. He raises no objection. I'm on duty, one ear cocked, one eye open, even so, on hand in case I'm needed.'

Waters tapped the sheet of paper in front of him, in which the porter's statement had been taken earlier by another officer.

'There's just one bit of clarification I want. I'm sure you're aware we've now interviewed all the residents in the hotel, and most of the staff. There's one person we haven't spoken to, a lady who signed the register as … ah … Eileen Grant. There's no record of her checking out, I see.'

The night porter shrugged. 'Far as I know she didn't check out in the usual way. I spoke to the manager earlier. Seems she paid in advance for her room, so there was no real need, I suppose, for her to go through any other formalities. No need to go to the desk, when she decided to leave.'

'No, I suppose not, though it's a bit unusual. So you didn't see her leave the hotel?'

'I did not.'

Inspector Waters consulted the notes in front of him. 'But you had met her. It says here that you carried her case up to her room when she arrived. But that's during the day. How did that come about? You weren't on duty, I imagine.'

The night porter smoothed down the wing of grey hair at the side of his head. 'I had just taken my usual snack below stairs. I was on my way to the room I use when I saw her going up to her room. She didn't have much by way of luggage but I thought it would be the courteous thing to do, to offer assistance, show her to the room.'

Inspector Waters clearly felt it was sufficiently unusual for an off-duty staff member to behave in such a way to press the matter. 'Courteous, hey? Pretty, was she?'

The night porter was offended. 'She was, if you would like to know. But that was nothing to do with it. I've been in the business forty years. I believe certain things should be done properly, not because I'm paid to do them, but because it's right to behave like that. My father before me, he….' The old man frowned, realized he was wandering. 'And as I already told you, her luggage, the case, it was just an overnight bag really, light, probably carrying just flimsy night clothes, that sort of thing. It didn't break my back to help.'

'I see…. Anyway, it seems she stayed in her room most of the time.'

'I can't confirm that, Inspector. I wasn't on duty.'

'You stated here you saw the woman a couple of times in the evening.'

The porter nodded. 'I was off duty, but I was pottering around, having a meal. And later on I went for my usual evening constitutional, a stroll across the bridge. It's pleasant doing that, a little evening air before I take up my duties again.'

Inspector Waters leaned forward, elbows on the table between them. 'And you came across her outside. So precisely where did you see her?'

The porter wrinkled his nose. 'First time I saw her she was standing outside the hotel, on the garden path. I nodded to her when I walked past, and she recognized me, smiled but said nothing.'

'What was she doing there?' Waters demanded.

'In the garden? Admiring the scenery, I suppose.'

'You suppose?'

The porter shrugged. 'Well, she was standing there, looking out towards the river and the road.'

'Not strolling.'

The porter hesitated, then shook his grey head. 'No, just standing there. On reflection, you could say she might have been sort of hanging around.'

'You mean she was waiting for someone? You didn't mention that earlier when you made a statement.'

'Well, no. Hadn't thought about it, really. But who can say?' He considered the matter for a few seconds, shaking his head slowly. 'It's just that I didn't think about it much at the time, but looking back maybe she *was* watching for someone, a car or something, or expected to meet someone. I don't know. I wasn't paying that much attention.'

Inspector Waters was unhappy. His tone had become irritated. 'When was the next time you saw her?'

'Maybe an hour later, when I was walking back to the hotel after my stroll. That time she was on the terrace. She was casually walking around as though she was enjoying the evening air but again, who knows? She *could* have been keeping an eye on the road and the bridge and the cars passing by, that sort of thing.'

'And according to your statement, you saw her again later?'

'I did. Pretty late it was then. I was on duty then, and I was going through to the kitchen to pick up the snack they lay out for me. I caught sight of her going into the residents' lounge. That was about eleven, and I think she must have ordered a drink because the barman was still on duty.'

'And that was the last you saw of her?' the inspector asked brusquely, slipping the statement into a file cover, clearly regarding the interview at an end.

'That it was. But I remember thinking that if things were as they looked she'd—'

'That's fine, thank you.' The inspector interrupted him, tossed the file aside, yawned, flexed his shoulder muscles.

The porter began to rise, his mouth set in a line, probably slightly offended by the manner in which the inspector had cut him off. Grout knew that the inspector would probably be less than pleased if he stepped in but nevertheless he said quietly, 'I'm sorry, sir, but could I have a word?' Before waiting for permission, he spoke to the porter. 'What were you about to say "if things were as they looked"?'

Inspector Waters was glaring at Grout with steely eyes. But he said in a cold voice, 'Yes, tell us what you were about to say.'

The porter was aware of the sudden drop in temperature between the two officers. But it wasn't his business. 'Well, you see, like I said she was a handsome woman, and not beyond reacting to a man if you know what I mean. So when I saw her there, it occurred to me that he might make a move on her, the way he was trying to catch her eye. I don't know if he managed it, of course, I wasn't aware of any room prowling if you get my drift—'

'What the hell are you talking about?' the inspector snapped.

'I'm talking about the other guest in the lounge.'

'The other guest? You made no mention of him in your statement.'

'Wasn't asked, was I?'

The inspector glanced angrily at Grout and then demanded of the night porter, 'This other guest … who was it?'

'The single gentleman,' the porter said sturdily. 'I mean, there was a group in from Newcastle that night, cricket club lot I believe, and they were a bit noisy in the bar but it wasn't one of them, though if they'd have seen her I don't doubt one of them would have chanced his arm. But they'd gone by then.'

'The single individual,' Waters prompted with an irritated sigh.

'It was Mr Gilbert, of course. He'd been staying here for a few days. The one who found the body down at Chesters this morning. He was going into the lounge, and it looked to me like he was hoping to join her. I heard later, when I was chatting to the barman, that he'd paid for her drink, so maybe he knew her, maybe they was acquainted, but what happened after I saw him go into the lounge, I don't know. Not surprising though, she was a bonny girl.'

After the porter had left the room, the inspector drew the file towards him and stared at it. Bright red spots were burning on his cheeks and he kept his head down when he spoke.

'I did point out you had no standing here, Detective Sergeant Grout.'

'You did, sir.'

'So keep your nose out of it.'

'I—'

'I'd have got around to that bit of information in due course,'

Waters announced severely. 'But it's *our* job to carry out these interrogations, not yours, so if you are going to stick around, keep your mouth shut. You're an observer, nothing more.'

He stood up, marched across the room, flung open the door and ordered the constable in the corridor to get hold of Paul Gilbert. He came back in, sat down, ignored Grout and stared at his hands laid flat on the table in front of him. The silence grew around them, edged with hostility. Grout wondered why the inspector was so touchy but he stepped back to lean against the wall when the door finally opened and Paul Gilbert entered.

Grout eyed him curiously.

The man was perhaps thirty-five or forty years of age. His features were lean, tanned and his eyes were quick and grey. His hair was sandy in colour, neatly smoothed back and there was a hint of encroaching baldness at the temples and also at the crown of his head. He was a man who was careful about his appearance, Grout guessed; he wore an expensive shirt, open at the neck with a silk scarf knotted at the throat. His trousers were pale blue, his shoes pale brown corduroy. Grout felt it was a curiously effeminate outfit. The man's fingers, laced together as he sat down in front of Inspector Waters, were slim.

'Mr Paul Gilbert. It says here in your statement that you're a photographer.'

'That's right.'

'And an author.'

'Correct. You have this on file now, don't you? And I've already made a statement. What more do I need to add?' Gilbert sounded irritated.

The inspector's eyes were hostile as he looked at the silk scarf Gilbert affected. 'These books you write … they wouldn't be about sex and violence, that sort of thing?'

'Hardly,' Gilbert drawled easily. 'I produce photographic essays, and before you jump to the wrong conclusion they do not include what some describe as art shots.'

'Naked birds, you mean?' the inspector asked insolently.

'If you so wish to describe them. No, I do not photograph nubile young women in states of undress. My books are mainly of landscapes. I did a successful publication last year based on the West Riding. I followed that with an exhibition of my work. In Leeds. At present I'm preparing a similar production on Northumberland and Hadrian's Wall. That's the reason for my presence at this hotel. But I've already told you all this. Or told one of your minions, anyway.'

'You *are* interested in sex, though,' Waters grunted provocatively.

Grout was beginning to think that the inspector's interviewing technique was almost antediluvian and certainly objectionable.

Gilbert's back stiffened. 'What on earth do you mean by that remark?'

'Women. You're interested in women.'

Gilbert blinked. 'Who isn't? Yes, I have a healthy interest in the other sex, as you also probably do, Inspector.'

'My inclinations are not in question here! Are you married?'

Paul Gilbert's eyes narrowed. 'No, I am not.'

'But you have girlfriends, is that right?'

'No steady partner, if that's what you mean.' Gilbert's tone hardened. 'What's this got to do with my finding that body at Chesters this morning?'

'Don't know yet. But why didn't you tell us about picking up that woman last night in the lounge?'

There was a short silence. At last, Gilbert said, 'I resent the tone of your voice, Inspector. I've been asked about, and made a statement concerning what I found this morning. That's the only relevant matter, it seems to me, that can help in your enquiries. And I resent the manner in which you seem to want to trawl through my private business.'

Inspector Waters leaned back in his chair and locked his hands behind his head. 'Come on, Gilbert, let's have it out in the open. There was a woman here last night. She registered herself as Eileen Grant. You were trying to have it off with her, weren't you?'

'What are you talking about?'

'You paid for her drink in the bar, chatted her up. Followed her into the residents' lounge. Late in the evening. What happened after that?'

'It's none of your damned business!' Gilbert snapped angrily.

Grout felt that Inspector Waters seemed to have touched a raw nerve in the photographer.

'I repeat, it's none of your business! But I've nothing to conceal. Yes, I met her and I paid for her drink. Yes, we had a brief conversation in the lounge. Then we went to our respective rooms. I didn't see her again after that. She did not appear at breakfast. And that's all I can tell you about her.'

There was anger in his tone, but something else again, Grout suspected. A suppressed irritation, a frustration. Maybe Gilbert had tried to pick up the Grant woman. From his bitter tone, Grout wondered whether the attempt had been unsuccessful.

After a moment, Gilbert muttered, 'Yes, we talked in the lounge. And then, after a while, after we had a drink together I went onto the terrace. She was there too. We spoke there for a while. A few minutes only, until she finished her drink. Then she left to go to her room, I stayed on the terrace. That was it.'

The inspector nodded. Grout felt he should be pressing the

matter a little further, less suggestively perhaps, but it seemed that Waters was losing interest in this line of inquiry. He was looking back at the notes taken in Gilbert's earlier interview. Grout would have liked to intervene but had already been told to back off once. He was disinclined to raise the inspector's blood pressure further.

'Let's turn to other matters. Your statement ...' Inspector Waters said. 'You say you found the body up at Chesters when you were out walking?'

'Yes.'

'You always go for a walk before breakfast?'

Paul Gilbert hesitated slightly. Grout felt the man would have liked to say it was his normal habit, but decided against it.

'No ... but, well, I couldn't sleep. Had a bad night.'

'Because of the alcohol you'd drunk?'

Gilbert raised his head disdainfully. 'No. It was insomnia. I had little to drink that evening. But I had things on my mind.'

'The woman?' Waters demanded, almost sneering.

Gilbert bridled. 'I was lying awake, planning my photographic layouts. It can get ... obsessive.'

'So there was no particular reason why you wandered in the direction of Chesters?'

'One can obtain interestingly lit shots in the early morning.'

'So you took your camera.'

Gilbert hesitated. 'No, I didn't.'

Waters looked him directly in the eyes. 'Funny, though. You aren't a habitual morning stroller. You go out, without your camera. And you find a dead man. Pity ... still, it's your loss, isn't it? You could have taken a shot the newspapers would have paid a bundle for. I think that's something you must regret now, hey? But by the way, did you take a shot of that woman, Eileen Grant?'

There was a short silence.

'I did not,' Gilbert said at last.

Once again, Grout had the instinctive feeling there was something Paul Gilbert was holding back. It was nothing he could put his finger on but he felt there was an odd undercurrent, a tension behind the man's words. Grout glanced at Inspector Waters; it seemed the thought had not occurred to him. Grout opened his mouth and then, once again, thought better of it.

Inspector Waters tossed aside the statement that Gilbert had provided. He looked at his own notes. 'All right, Mr Gilbert, we'll leave it at that. If you'd be so kind to make a further statement regarding your meeting with Eileen Grant we needn't bother you further.'

Gilbert's chair scraped as he stood up. He stood there for a moment, looking down at the police inspector. 'Why are you so interested in Eileen Grant? Why all the questions about her?'

Inspector Waters smiled thinly. 'We're simply following up on anything of interest, Mr Gilbert. Just make the statement. Add perhaps what you and she talked about, that sort of thing.'

'She said little. We just talked about my work.'

'There you are then. That tells us something, doesn't it? She's interested in photography!'

Gilbert scowled. 'It was just a casual conversation. But I don't understand … You're suggesting some kind of link. What has she got to do with all this … business?' He could not bring himself to mention the dead man he had stumbled across at Chesters.

Inspector Waters gathered up his papers. His tone was cool. 'We don't know yet. The fact is, this lady friend of yours, she upped and left early this morning, it seems. Sort of … disappeared. Maybe around the time you were taking a stroll and finding yourself staring at over a corpse. Or maybe she left earlier. You see, Mr Gilbert, there's a sort of mystery about our Miss Eileen Grant. But we'll find out in due course. We'll find out, I'm sure....'

Detective Chief Inspector James Cardinal arrived in Newcastle early that evening. Rooms had been booked for him and for Grout at the Turks Head Hotel. Grout met the senior officer in the bar before dinner. Cardinal ordered drinks for them both, and after a brief hesitation told the barman to put the tab on his room. Grout guessed the hesitation was due to Cardinal's hope that Grout would dig into his own pocket for the drinks. It was a game of cat and mouse that Grout had become accustomed to playing; he knew that if he waited, Cardinal would give in. It was a minor triumph but one he enjoyed.

'I've had a long talk with the Chief Constable,' Cardinal said. He sipped his Newcastle Brown and pulled a lugubrious face. 'Strong stuff, this ... I spent the afternoon with him at Ponteland and put him in the picture. It's what I expected. I had to work on him a while before he agreed we could continue an involvement in the investigation into Rigby's murder. He says his own people have plenty on their plates anyway.'

Grout had little doubt Inspector Waters would be less than pleased.

'We can have the use of the lab facilities up at Gosforth,' Cardinal continued. 'Any other help we need, we can just ask for it.'

'I doubt if the lower ranks will go along with that willingly,' Grout observed.

'Touchy, are they? Well, it's to be expected, I suppose. So your visit to Chesters wasn't all wine and roses?'

'Truculence was in the air,' Grout admitted.

'Truculence.' Cardinal registered that he was impressed by the choice of word. Then he grinned. He was in an expansive mood. He could remember that not so long ago Grout had been a member of a provincial force and would have bitterly resented the entry of an outsider to his manor. Shows how situations can alter feelings, he concluded to himself. 'So where do you go from here?' Cardinal asked.

'There are several questions I want to ask witnesses … they'll have dispersed so I'll have to chase them up.'

'Legwork's good for you, lad,' Cardinal said approvingly. 'Get you away from those books you stick your head into. You're a copper, not a lawyer. Anyway, fill me in with what you've got.'

Grout did so, telling him what had happened at Chesters and at The George Hotel.

'So, you think this woman—'

'Eileen Grant. At least, that's how she registered herself at the hotel. Could be an assumed name, of course.'

'You think she might possibly be tied up in the murder?'

'That's going a bit too far, sir, at the moment. But it's a possibility. All this hanging around outside the hotel … it could be she was waiting for someone, and that person could be Rigby. Or maybe she was waiting to meet the man who killed him.'

Cardinal grimaced. 'That's all going a bit too far for my money.'

'She left the hotel without checking out.'

Cardinal nodded, frowned. 'We'll need to ask her about that when we find her. But you think this man Gilbert has more to tell us?'

Grout nodded. 'I'd like to have another word with him. I have the feeling there's something he was holding back. But I don't know what, and it may not be important. Still ...'

They were silent for a little while. Cardinal employed himself by steadily emptying his glass. Then he stared at it, raised his eyes to Grout, and scowled until Grout took the message.

'Same again, sir?'

'No,' he replied, to Grout's relief. The relief was short-lived. 'No, I'll have a Jameson this time. Double. I'm partial to Irish whiskey, even if I have no great love for the Irish themselves. All that peat, and mournful songs and mountains sweeping down to the sea.'

'Well, you have to admit they built our railways,' Grout said. He rose, went to the bar and obtained the drinks, settling for another half of Newcastle Brown for himself. When he returned, Cardinal accepted the glass and said reflectively, 'Leave this woman – Grant – to me. We've got her description, I'll get it circulated. The address she gave on the register might not check out, but we'll see.'

'What about the photographer, Gilbert?'

'We'll let him stew a few days. Don't push him. If he's got more to tell us, pressure right now might make him dig in his heels but if he's left alone, given time to cool down, thinks he's clear, a bit of verbal needling later on might cause him to collapse. That's called psychology, Grout.'

Cod psychology, Grout thought to himself, but remained silent.

'Then there's the other question to consider,' Cardinal murmured.

'The museum?' Grout suggested.

'Exactly that,' Cardinal nodded. 'We need to find out why it got broken into. Was it Rigby himself who broke in? And if so, what the hell was he after? Apart from which, what was a fairly well-provided art thief, working for my old friend Gus Clifford, doing out at Chesters in the first place?'

'He was supposed to have been on his way to London for the meeting,' Grout said. 'I've been puzzling about that myself. Did he know the meeting had been cancelled?'

Cardinal sipped his whiskey with an air of considerable satisfaction, partly because it was a Jameson, and partly, Grout guessed, because he had not paid for it himself.

'I'd be prepared to bet that Gus Clifford's fingers are all over this business. I'd bet my bottom dollar on it. But what I can't work out is what would be in the museum at Chesters to pull Rigby there, never mind why he got murdered for his pains. Was Rigby obeying orders from his boss, or did he get turned off because he was trying to strike out on his own? You find out, Grout, and who knows? I might even put it in your case for promotion.'

That old carrot again, Grout thought. 'The curator told me the man who heads the Antiquities section at the university knows as much about that storeroom as anyone. He often takes students there with him, as part of their training. I think my first task had better be to have a word with him. Find out what he can tell me. The curator says the man is well-known to the general public. His name is Professor Godfrey.'

Cardinal frowned. 'Godfrey? I fancy I've come across that name somewhere.' Then he recollected; his wife watched popular television programmes about archaeology, and often drooled about a professor called Godfrey. 'He wouldn't be the one who appears on television programmes, would he?'

'Don't know, sir.'

'That's right,' Cardinal said sourly. 'Law, not archaeology, is your thing. God knows what you hope to get out of all that study. Law, and Urdu ... Still, it'll be up your street, prowling around the university corridors, hob-nobbing with those young oiks and their stuck up teachers, dons, whatever they call themselves. Did I ever tell you I never went to university, Grout?'

Mentally, Grout groaned. He suspected Cardinal was going to talk about the University of Life.

'I'm a graduate of the University of Life, me.'

Cardinal rose to his feet, a tall, slim man with the beginnings of a middle-aged paunch. Two inches shorter, younger, thicker in the body and slower in his movements, Grout scrambled to his feet. Cardinal eyed him carefully.

'You knew I was going to say that, didn't you, Grout?'

Grout hesitated, then shrugged non-committally.

'Smartarse,' Cardinal said and led the way from the bar towards the dining room. 'You can buy the wine.'

CHAPTER FOUR

Detective Sergeant Grout was never quite certain about the nature of his relationship with Chief Inspector Cardinal.

The DCI had made no direct reference to the fact that it had been the Chief Constable, Grout's uncle who had recommended that Grout be attached to Cardinal's squad but there had been the occasional barbed comment, hints that the DCI disliked suggestions of nepotism. On the other hand, Grout felt that Cardinal had been impressed by the assistance he had been able to provide in the first case they had worked together. The closing of the illegal immigrant case in Bradford had been facilitated by Grout's ability to communicate with the local community, not least because he was able to converse with them in Urdu. Not that it had prevented Cardinal from continuing to make a few snide comments from time to time about Grout's activities outside his mainstream occupation as a detective; the DCI had made it clear he felt Grout's law studies – and even the acquisition of Urdu – were largely a distraction, or even a waste of time. Though there were occasions when Grout suspected Cardinal quietly approved of the fact he was trying to extend his qualifications, even if he would never admit to the fact.

What puzzled Grout, and somewhat disoriented him, was that Cardinal also seemed to put as many obstacles in his way as he possibly could, restricting the time he had available to study – albeit while rightly insisting that his full-time job with the Squad must come first. But it all led to a confusion in Grout's mind: he could not work out just what Cardinal really felt about him. As a colleague, and as a man.

What was certainly clear was the fact that Cardinal was determined to get the last ounce of effort out of Grout in the carrying out of his duties.

Grout's appointment to meet Professor Godfrey at the university was quickly made. When he arrived at the professor's office he recognized him immediately as a man who had made frequent television appearances, even though Grout would have been unable to identify the programmes in which the academic had appeared. It was a comment he was sorry he made, when he blurted it out to the professor.

'Ah yes,' Godfrey said, nodding his head and laughing in a somewhat falsely embarrassed fashion which Grout felt was a little theatrical, 'it's one of the problems associated with the media spotlight. Being recognized in the street and yet being taken for some other celebrity – not, of course, that I really regard myself as a celebrity! In addition, I've come to realize that the academic world being what it is, one loses a certain amount of credibility among colleagues if one appears too often. A panel game for morons and a tutorial or lecture presentation before some of the best brains in university circles ... some people regard these as occupations that are, shall we say, mutually exclusive.'

Godfrey was a few inches taller than Grout, broad-shouldered, immaculately dressed in an elegantly cut grey suit.

His features were finely-chiselled, good-humoured and as he spoke he leant forward as though wishing to build personal bridges with the person he was talking to. His brown hair curled thickly on the top of his head but at the temples there was a frosting of silver. Women would find this man attractive and television appearances would enhance his insistently sincere gaze.

Indeed, Grout wondered whether Godfrey's personal appeal had been remodelled, chiselled out of his experiences in front of the camera. Certainly, the professor was a personable individual; he was reputed to receive considerable fan mail for his Sunday afternoon cultural programmes, and the inanities of the panel game he chaired on Tuesday evenings would seem to fix millions in their armchairs. He was unmarried and his secretary clearly adored him, as did many of the middle-aged women who were addicted to his appearances. As they sat in the Senior Common Room Godfrey offered Grout a drink. Grout refused, he had a suspicion it might be sherry. Courteously, when Grout refused the offer, Godfrey refrained from calling for a drink for himself.

'I don't get too much hassle from my colleagues at the university here, about my television appearances, I mean,' Godfrey announced, crossing one leg over the other as he settled back into his leather armchair. 'A certain amount of chaffing goes on, naturally, it's understandable. The thing is, as long as one maintains a reasonable academic reputation with published works, it's possible to keep the critics at bay. I get a few snide remarks in the press thrown at me from time to time, but one must develop a thick skin to ward off such gnat bites, don't you agree?'

Grout had never appeared on television, and did not expect to do so. But he agreed with the comment. It was difficult to do otherwise with this charming and easy-mannered man.

'I understand one of your published works concerns Chesters Fort,' Grout said.

'Oh, it wasn't just about Chesters,' the professor replied swiftly. 'The book was rather wider in concept than that. It ranged across the whole raft of reasons for the building of the original Wall, the legions that built it, the pinnacle of its utility, its gradual abandonment and decay … no, the book did not concentrate merely on Chesters. On the other hand, you might be referring to the slighter book on Chesters itself, that was merely an extract from the major work … there was a local print run from a small Chester-le-Street publisher that was quite successful. I have a copy or two in my room, I'll let you have a signed copy if you would like one.'

Non-committally, Grout replied, 'That's very kind, Professor.' He paused. 'You'll have heard about the murder up at Chesters.'

'My dear chap,' Godfrey spread his well-manicured hands theatrically, 'when the news broke, I was one of the first people local television contacted to obtain some background and local colour. They didn't actually use me personally in the presentation but … well, the event has set things buzzing in the north, hasn't it? So *romantic*, after all, a murder at such an historic site.'

There had been nothing romantic about the flies buzzing around Rigby's smashed skull, but Grout did not give voice to the thought. Godfrey smiled his easy, understanding smile.

'I've no doubt you would see things in quite a different light, of course. But you must remember we all have our personal perspectives. As an historian I am always tempted to take the long term view, place matters in their historical context. My public career, enhanced and perhaps, I admit, somewhat twisted by the demands of the media upon my time, has emerged from the romantic mists that antiquity bestows upon what many regard as the mundane. Of course, this has brought me considerable financial rewards and allowed me to build up my own personal collection of interesting artefacts of historical value. But in short, I believe in the *drama* of history.'

Codswallop, Grout thought.

'Even yesterday's history,' Godfrey continued in a thoughtful tone. 'Which is, of course, really why you wanted to talk with me. So, forgive me, enough inconsequential chatter. In what manner may I be able to help you?'

Grout was becoming somewhat irritated by the hint of condescension in Godfrey's tone and the rather portentous phrasing he used. Bluntly, he said, 'I want to hear about your Student Survey Group, and the work you've done at Chesters.'

'Really?' Godfrey seemed surprised. 'I can't see what my little student group would have to do with a murdered man up at Chesters.'

'It's just in the way of general enquiries,' Grout grunted. 'I need to fill in some background stuff.'

Godfrey twisted his mouth in a grimace of concerned consideration. 'Of course, Detective Sergeant, I understand. Well, let's see, I formed the group about four years ago. Since I took over as head of the Antiquities Department here, things have progressed rather well, even if I do say so myself. After I obtained my professorial chair and published my monograph on the Wall, the television work started and a number of research students were consequently attracted to the department. I suppose the media publicity drew them in, and perhaps the hope that they also might make the odd appearance on the box. Interesting, isn't it? What people will do to attain their brief moments of fame....'

'The work you did at Chesters,' Grout reminded the self-satisfied academic.

'Ah yes, well, it seemed to me it would be worthwhile to introduce new students to the beauty and thrill of archaeology by letting them handle and deal with items that were stored at Chesters. It allowed them to develop instincts for the dating of artefacts, to make allowances for the feel of history under their clumsy hands, to inculcate in them an understanding of workmanship and time and the endeavours of men who once trod these hills but have now vanished into dust....' Godfrey's glance fixed on Grout's. He became aware of the frown on the detective sergeant's brow. He shrugged. 'The idea was simple and, I admit, not new. But it helped the students develop documentation, identify locations, look for signs of archaeological interest, and took them into the realms of historical records, parish registers which are now available online, classical accounts... In reality, I had a fairly Catholic view of the activity of the group. Anything that might add to our store of knowledge, and enhance the student understanding of history, it was all grist to our mill.'

'I understand you had groups of students working at the museum at Chesters.'

'Naturally. Among other sites of historical interest. I don't imagine you'll wish to interview any of them about it, however. They'll have nothing to impart which I can't cover. I keep a close eye on all that's gone on in the museum. It's a matter of responsibility, don't you know?' Abruptly, he rose and smiled. 'But you never know, do you?' He gestured towards the door. 'Come. I'll take you downstairs, introduce you to Dobson.'

Aaron Dobson turned out to be a somewhat pimply young man who was prematurely bald. He was probably no more than twenty-five years of age but his pate shone, shaven in an attempt to hide his baldness. Grout was reminded of a pink billiard ball. Dobson was a rather nervous young man who kept stroking his eyebrows as though assuring himself they at least were still there. His glance was quick and agitated, his hands rarely still.

Godfrey introduced him as the current student leader of the group. Grout assumed it would have been on account of his intellectual abilities rather than his leadership qualities, for Dobson seemed to be in an almost constant state of terror in his struggle to face the world of his choosing.

Professor Godfrey suggested Grout might question Dobson alone since he had work to do. He left, after stating he would be happy to speak further with Grout later, in the privacy of his office, if that was what Grout desired.

'Yeah, that's right, we've been working up at Chesters on and off for a couple of years now,' Dobson stated after the professor had left. 'It's not had a high priority in the department, I mean, the museum is the kind of resource we can use from time to time, particularly with the new research students who come into the department each year.' He glanced nervously around the room, as though wishing Professor Godfrey had not left him alone. 'It can get pretty boring from time to time,' he admitted.

Grout wondered whether he would have said that if Godfrey had been present.

'So, while working in the museum storeroom did you develop notes ... or a record of the items down there?' Grout asked. 'The curator seemed a bit vague about it, he didn't really seem to know what was stored there.'

Dobson gave his left eyebrow a little tug. 'We do, yeah, because of the young students we have working there. You got to keep tabs on things, don't you? There's a handout for instance, we made it up for the Ministry of Works, though it didn't include everything. Our own records are more detailed, and some of the items we list we're not sure about, dating, provenance, that sort of thing. You see, the problem is—'

'What I'm really interested in,' Grout interrupted, daunted by the imminent flow of irrelevant information Dobson was likely to produce, 'is just a list of the storeroom contents.'

Dobson blinked. His fingers wandered up to his eyebrow again, but he restrained himself. 'The stuff in the basement, yeah. We kept some records. But apart from our general list I don't think there's much we can do to help.'

'You haven't a complete list?' Grout asked in surprise. 'Neither you nor the curator—'

Dobson shuffled uncertainly, cast a glance at the ceiling as though seeking assistance. 'Well, it's been kind of low priority, you understand. Some of the stuff has been identified, written up, because if we have a student who's specializing in a research programme the chances are he or she will have done some close rooting around and will want to record what they've found. The storeroom contents, well, we've all been involved in that but the general view is that there's not much down there which is of significant interest. If it was, it wouldn't be down there. It'd be upstairs, wouldn't it?'

Grout sighed. He had the feeling he was wading around in a field of thick mud, getting nowhere. Nevertheless, he had to admit Dobson was probably right. So the question remained: why was the museum broken into, by Rigby or by his killer? If nothing appeared to have been taken from the upper rooms, why had anyone bothered to break in if there was nothing worthwhile stealing in the storeroom?

'On the other hand, now I think about it,' Dobson

murmured, creasing his brow thoughtfully, 'it could be I'm not exactly right.'

'What's that supposed to mean?' Grout asked, puzzled.

'Well, like I said, we've been working at Chesters for a few years and the team's changed over that time, as students have come in, moved off, taken up other projects, so when I spoke I was thinking about the *present* team, of course.'

'Of course,' Grout repeated, not understanding what Dobson was talking about.

'I said a moment ago, we each had sort of special interests, the ones who worked at Chesters. There was Phil Proud, for instance, a while ago. His special interest was thirteenth century. Not just Britain. European stuff as well.'

'Phil Proud.'

'That's the man. He was on the team a year or so ago before he moved on. I seem to recall that when he was rooting around in the basement he did some cataloguing. And more than that, he seemed to spend more time there than we would have expected.'

'Are you suggesting he might have made a more detailed analysis of the stuff down there than you or the curator might have done?'

'Something like that,' Dobson replied, somewhat defensively.

'Where can I find him?' Grout asked.

'No idea. He's no longer at the university. He sort of got thrown out.' Dobson grimaced, then corrected himself. 'Not thrown out exactly. He was awarded his MA and off he went, although there was an expectation he would have been staying on to do his Ph.D and then perhaps be taken on in the department as a researcher. That was the chat among the students anyway. He was a bright lad. But there was some sort of kerfuffle, I don't know, bit of trouble about his thesis, he lost it or something, but it was Professor Godfrey who pulled the rabbit out of the hat.'

'How do you mean?' Grout asked, even more puzzled.

'The prof fought Proud's corner. He pushed his case. The prof's a good guy, you know? He argued with the Senate and got them to award the degree even though something had happened to the thesis. But the prof can tell you all about that. Maybe he can even tell you where Proud ended up. Sorry I can't be of more help, man.'

There was something about Dobson's manner of speaking which made Grout feel the man had not outgrown his youth. Perhaps he was fated to remain in the time warp that was the university department of Archaeology.

Professor Godfrey lounged back in his chair, flicked a spot of lint from his cuff and smiled at Grout as he waved him to a seat beside the mullioned window in his small office.

'Yes, I thought there wouldn't be a great deal of assistance you would be able to get from the department staff. You must realize, Sergeant, that all our staff exist in their own little worlds. They are academics, or budding academics, and they are obsessed with their fields of specialism. Little interests them beyond that, other than the usual things like beer and girls. The single ones, anyway. Though I suspect the few married ones among them also have those external … well, maybe I shouldn't go there. No, their lives are largely dictated by the range of their work: exhibits at a museum, learned writings, ancient documents, crouching over laptops in search of esoteric items of information online … they don't find much to interest them in an out of the way storeroom.'

Grout sat down on the chair facing the professor, after first removing several books and placing them on the floor beside the chair. Sunlight lanced through the rather dirty window and he was aware of the distant sound of traffic funnelling up from the Haymarket. He remained silent for a little while.

'So is there anything else we can help you with?' Professor Godfrey queried.

'Dobson mentioned a former student of yours, by the name of Phil Proud.'

Grout could not be entirely certain, but he felt he detected a certain change in Godfrey's hitherto easy manner. His glance flickered around the room as he seemed to hesitate, collecting his thoughts, marshalling his thought processes. He rose to his feet, turned to look out of the window, peering through the grime to the streets below. 'Philip Proud.' There was a certain hesitancy in his tone.

'Dobson reckoned Proud spent more time in the Chesters storeroom than was usual among your students. Does that mean Proud might have developed a list of the holdings, a catalogue of some sort?'

Godfrey shrugged, turned back from the window, settling himself once more in his chair. He shuffled some papers on his desk in front of him, almost absent-mindedly. 'That may well be so, though it's something that hasn't previously come to my attention. In fact, I'm somewhat surprised to hear of it. Chesters was a Roman fort, the antiquities were discovered there, they were almost all artefacts from the Roman period, some valuable, some run of the mill, so to speak. But Proud's interests were related to a different area of study, he was interested in a study of the thirteenth century in Europe, that disastrous epoch when so much collapsed, values were questioned, religion and superstition and raw ambitions raged out of control in civilized societies ... if you could call them

77

civilized.' He paused, smiled deprecatingly. 'Sorry, I'm begin-
ning to sound like a television script, aren't I? Rooting around
Chesters would have been a waste of time for young Proud.
Maybe that's why he ended up the way he did.'

Grout seemed to detect an irritated disapproval in the
professor's tone.

'Weren't you his supervisor?'

Godfrey spread his hands in an ineffectual gesture. 'Of
course, but one can't always keep close track … and in many
ways it's important that students seek their own byways to
reach the goals they aspire to. Perhaps I should have directed
him more closely? Maybe that's true. But one has only so much
time, and there are one's own interests to consider …'

Like television appearances, Grout thought.

Godfrey took a deep, considered breath. 'But let me be clear.
Proud was a good student. And perhaps I set my standards
too high. He was good, but in the long run I suppose I have to
admit that I found his work … somewhat disappointing.'

'Why was that?'

'I hesitate to explain. It's a long story.'

'Give me a summary.'

Godfrey grimaced, took a deep breath. 'If you wish. Philip
Proud came to the university to read for his first degree.
History. He took a First and when he asked if I would take
him on as a research student while he read for his Masters, by
thesis, I agreed. He seemed good material. The field he wished
to undertake research into, well, it wasn't my specialist area,
but there are always colleagues one can refer to, and he seemed
bright, so I agreed.'

'What particular field was he interested in?'

'Mediaeval Italy. Firenze and the Borgias. Blood-letting and
murder. Power struggles and the explosion of mediaeval art.

All very exciting and romantic. I was impressed by his enthu-
siasm. Of course, it's not my field so there was not a lot I could
do to direct his studies, but I did what I could to help.'

'Even when he got into some kind of trouble with his thesis?'

Godfrey raised an eyebrow, and stared at Grout. Then he
nodded. 'How would you know...? Ah, of course. Dobson
would have mentioned that.' The professor gave a reluctant
shrug. 'It was not exactly trouble. More, it was some kind of
falling off with his work ethic in the first instance. He worked
well enough at the beginning, indeed, for most of the year, but
then somehow he seemed to slack off. He missed a few of his
tutorials with me, was absent for a period from the campus.
I cornered him at one point, asked him what was going on,
tried to discover if there was a problem I could help deal with.
I got the impression it was probably a personal matter ... the
usual thing. I came to the conclusion there was a girl in the
background.' Godfrey smiled ruefully. 'Not an uncommon
experience, of course. We've all been there, isn't that so?' When
Grout made no reply, Godfrey went on, 'So there wasn't much
I could do. Other than to offer some fatherly advice. And to be
honest, even though he was, well, not slacking, but being less
committed, what I saw of his written work was still well up to
the standard I would have expected, and called for. In fact his
raw thesis was good. It needed polishing, of course, and some
of his references required further elucidation and support, but
I considered that on the whole it was a sound piece of research
and well worth publication. Not that it was ever published,
unfortunately.'

'Why was that?'

Godfrey was silent for a little while. His fingers teased at
one of the documents on the desk in front of him. 'It seems he
lost his thesis.'

'Lost it?'

'It got lost, or destroyed, burned … I can't quite recall the details but the point was he couldn't present the final version to the Senate. By carelessness, or whatever it was, he was throwing away his chance of obtaining his degree, and he seemed to wish to offer no reasonable explanation for it at all.'

'So he gave no explanation as to how the thesis was lost?'

'Not really. Or I should say, not convincingly. Lost, mislaid, destroyed … I always had a suspicion that he was telling me only half the story, stepping away from the truth. He came up with some vague litany of events, how he'd left his rooms unlocked, how other students may have raided it as some sort of prank in a drunken foray, they trashed his place and in the process his thesis went missing. He alluded vaguely to certain other students with whom he was not popular but there was nothing concrete to go on, it seems the printed materials he held had been burned, and—'

'Did he not have a copy on his computer?'

Godfrey eyed him, eyebrows raised. 'Ah, well, it seems that his laptop, which contained the details of his research, the master copy of his thesis and all his references, also got trashed. Or disappeared. As I say, I can't quite recall the details.'

'But you suggest you thought he wasn't telling you the whole story. Did you have any thoughts about what really might have happened?'

Godfrey wrinkled his brow, smoothed one hand carefully along the side of his head. 'One doesn't wish to enquire too deeply into personal matters. But I came to the conclusion it was all tied up with the … attachment he had developed. The girl he was dating, or living with, I don't know, it wasn't for me to pry, my guess was that they had had a violent quarrel, something had gone wrong, she trashed his manuscript and maybe made off with, or threw his laptop in the Tyne, I don't know.... Perhaps he hadn't been giving her the attention she thought she deserved. Perhaps there was something more serious. Maybe she wasn't a well-balanced young woman. Who knows? I didn't consider it was my business to investigate too closely.'

Grout frowned. 'But the upshot was a year's work was destroyed, and he had no thesis to present to the Senate.'

Godfrey sighed. 'That's about the size of it. There were a few scraps, bits and pieces relating to his research. And I had my own notes from the sessions we had together, when I was supervising his work, but let's put it like this, he was a foolish young man. He should have taken rather more precautions, in my view. I mean, it was all so ... irresponsible.'

'But I understand from Dobson that he was finally awarded his MA ... by your efforts, I believe,' Grout murmured.

Godfrey shrugged again and was silent for a little while. Grout waited. He thought about the influx of students to Godfrey's department and realized that the professor's treatment of Philip Proud would be symptomatic of the close regard the man had for his students. He would be popular for his extrovert manner and his television appearances but they would probably also respect him for the interest he took in their academic welfare ... and perhaps their personal lives.

Almost reluctantly, Godfrey murmured, 'I thought someone should fight his corner. He had worked hard; I didn't think it was right he should be penalized for some drunken prank by his fellow students. Or whatever it was ...'

'So what happened to him later? After he was awarded his MA, did Proud take up an academic appointment?' Grout asked.

'Did he hell! He threw away his future, dissipated his talents.' Godfrey's tone was wry, irritated, and Grout realized that there might be reasons other than those mentioned for Godfrey's disappointment in Philip Proud. He had helped the young man, nurtured his talent, assisted him towards the award of his MA in difficult circumstances, but there was something needling Godfrey about Philip Proud.

'So what happened to him after he left the university?'

'Do you know York?' Godfrey asked abruptly.

'Fairly well.'

'You'll know the Shambles then.'

'Most people do.'

The Shambles was the mediaeval street right in the centre of York with its overhanging windows, narrow street, lurching, crowded houses beloved by tourists. No longer the habitat of sellers of meat, it remained perhaps the most perfectly preserved mediaeval street in Britain.

'If you walk into the Shambles from the lower end – that's St. Hilary's end – you'll soon come across a small bookshop. If you were to put something completely out of character in that beautiful street, you'd install Philip Proud there. In pursuit of Venus, you might say. Selling cheap, salacious paperback books mainly for the shabby raincoat trade.'

His tones were edged with disgust. Grout could not be certain whether the disgust came from Proud's involvement with eroticism or simply with the book trade itself.

'So how did he come to set up there?" Grout asked.

'I understand he received some sort of legacy from a deceased aunt, but I've no idea how much it was, or indeed how he manages to keep his head above water financially, because I don't believe there's much trade for pornography down there in the Shambles. From what I hear the place is closed half the time anyway, and as for the present state the book trade finds itself in ... You know, if he had a legacy like that he could have done something useful with it, extended his learning, gone to Italy to do further research but instead of that the young fool deserted academia for the salacious end of the commercial world! Pornographic literature … and in the Shambles at that!'

It was clear to Grout that Godfrey regarded Proud's offence as even more heinous than allowing his precious thesis to have been destroyed. Grout was silent, making no attempt to sympathize, feeling that Proud was a young man making his own decisions for his own reasons; he was not to be bound by the desires and dictates of his older mentor. He glanced up and was surprised to see that Godfrey was staring at him with a half-smile on his face. It suggested to Grout that Godfrey was quite capable of self-analysis and was feeling slightly abashed at having expressed himself so forcibly.

'You must think I'm somewhat ivory-tower, and perhaps a certain … Victorian in my attitudes?'

'I think you were understandably disappointed, Professor Godfrey,' Grout replied non-committally.

'Yet who am I, really, to offer criticism?' Godfrey spread his hands wide in a somewhat theatrical gesture. 'After all, there are those I'm certain would rush to argue that I myself have prostituted my knowledge and talents to the ravening beast that is television. I suppose that's the trouble, really, university professors do live in a somewhat narrow world, and have difficulty seeing the wider issues … such as the need to earn a living. Maybe that's what drove Proud to his decision, though I can't believe he's making much success of his life on the road he's chosen for himself.…'

He nodded, hesitated, then raised his carefully trimmed eyebrows. He rose, moved towards the door, intimating the interview was at an end as far as he was concerned. 'I forget sometimes that I was once young too,' he murmured. 'But then, traditionally, all professors are forgetful, aren't they?'

So are detective sergeants, from time to time, Grout considered as he made his way down Blackett Street, away from the university. He realized he had forgotten to ask Professor Godfrey for the loan of the professor's monograph on Chesters Fort.

CHAPTER FIVE

Cardinal received Grout's report in silence. His lean, ascetic features remained impassive but Grout was in no doubt of the chief inspector's disapproval. He stumbled to the end of his account, stubbornly defiant in his tone of voice as he realized the extent of Cardinal's displeasure. Cardinal fixed a cold, contemptuous glance on the uncomfortable detective sergeant.

'So, it seems you had an enjoyable time fannying around, then?'

'I don't understand, sir.'

Cardinal allowed himself a thin smile; there was no warmth in it.

'As far as I can gather, you've been having a pleasant time swanning around York, chatting with a professor and a student while the rest of us have been keeping our noses to the grindstone. What your buggering about with academia has to do with the investigation we're carrying out, I haven't the faintest idea. Perhaps you could elucidate the point for me. Is that the right kind of academic phrase?'

Grout's chin came up stubbornly. 'Things might get a bit clearer when I've been allowed to interview Philip Proud, sir.'

'*Allowed*?' Cardinal's eyes widened in mock surprise. 'Seems to me you're wandering off on a frolic of your own with or without permission! As for this man Proud, you're not seriously suggesting you waste time talking to him about his lifestyle, his bloody thesis on mediaeval Italy, or whatever else you want to have a chat about. Or perhaps it's the pornography angle. It's not that you have a leaning towards dirty books, is it?'

Grout was annoyed. He felt he didn't deserve that kind of snide comment. Doggedly, he said, 'I just feel he might be able to help us with regard to why the Chesters storeroom was broken into.'

'I thought it just contained run of the mill stuff. So what will this bookseller have to tell us?'

'Until I speak to him, sir, how can we know?'

Grout sensed it was a standoff. But Cardinal was not the man to admit defeat. He shook his head sadly. 'You know, Grout, I sometimes despair about you. I can't see how Proud will be able to help us in the Rigby killing, or connections to Clifford, or anything else arising out of this bloody mess. From what you tell me, we don't even know whether Proud did any cataloguing in that storeroom, and even if he did, you'll tell me it was over a year ago. I just don't see what possible use ...'

Cardinal paused, considered matters. He stared at the young sergeant in front of him. He was sorely tempted to tell Grout that he should terminate the inquiry into the storeroom contents immediately. He should be concentrating on discovering who had killed Rigby rather than messing about with a break in at the museum which might have no connection whatsoever to Rigby. They didn't even know if anything had even been taken from the site ... or why Rigby was there in the first place. He was tempted ... but he hesitated.

It was not that Cardinal thought Grout might be right, and

on a useful track; he was fairly certain the sergeant was on a wild goose chase. On the other hand, since Grout had been working with him in the squad, Cardinal had become aware that Grout possessed a certain advantage over his superior officer. DCI Cardinal, he admitted wryly to himself, had always been a man who insisted on pursuing details, it was the way he had been trained. Doggedness was the key. But Grout was different. Cardinal sensed that the detective sergeant was a man to whom things happened, and his mind was of the kind that could leap into an abyss of indecision and reach surprising, and accurate conclusions. It was called flair, he supposed. Something he himself lacked.

Cardinal grunted sourly to himself. He knew he was a meticulous, plodding sort of copper – the results he achieved were usually a consequence of long, arduous, slogging drudgery. But Grout was of the kind to whom coincidence and accident were bedfellows. And he seemed to profit accordingly. After all, it was why Cardinal had accepted the recommendation from the Chief Constable – uncle or not – in the first instance. It was why he felt he needed Grout. Young blood. Natural intelligence. Lateral thinking. Uninhibited endeavour. He sighed. Maybe he should admit he and Grout could make a good combination: Cardinal to restrain Grout from his wilder flights; Grout to inject the unusual and unexpected into Cardinal's routine investigations.

The uneasy silence was finally broken by Grout clearing his throat nervously. He clearly felt the need to change the subject of their discussion. 'Have we got anything yet on the woman who was staying at the hotel, sir?'

Cardinal shook his head. 'Nothing yet. Her description has been circulated and I've got two men checking on likely female contacts of Rigby's. It seems,' he added bitterly, 'they have been rather numerous. Rigby should have been a sailor, in my view. He's docked in more than a few ports over the years.'

'How have they managed to check?' Grout asked.

'You mean what lines of inquiry have been followed? Apart from usual known acquaintances, the keys we found in Rigby's pocket were linked to a flat in Gosforth. Expensive place too, more than I could bloody afford. Anyway, there was some useful stuff there—'

'Do we have anything tying him in with Clifford?'

'Rigby wasn't stupid enough to leave anything of that kind lying around. But there were documents he was in the process of getting rid of, it seems. Papers had been dumped in the incinerator in the basement, but there were odd sheets that didn't get completely burned. Forensics had a crack at them and they think they'll manage to piece together some information from it all.'

'But you mentioned women friends.'

'Didn't get that from the papers that were dumped. No, much simpler. A diary in a bedroom drawer. Maybe he didn't think it was that important, or just forgot about it before he essayed forth into the night to get his skull crushed up at Chesters. No, there were a number of female acquaintances noted in his little black book. Unsurprisingly, some of them hookers. Others, well, they're being checked out but it would seem they could be simply casual acquaintances, girls he'd met in the clubs. Even just some personal friends. However, my guess is we'll find most of them are ... or were, rather ... in some sort of gainful employment with Rigby.'

Grout frowned. 'You mean a prostitution ring?'

'We'll wait and see. But Rigby was tied in with Gus Clifford, and that bastard was involved with women trafficking from Romania for a number of years.'

'So we might find the missing Miss Grant in there somewhere.'

Cardinal shrugged. 'Who knows? Under another name, maybe. Anyway, she's not turned up yet.'

'But what about the papers he was dumping? What importance did they have? And why would he try to get rid of them so suddenly?'

Cardinal shrugged. 'Something was panicking Rigby. He certainly wanted to get rid of some documents in his possession, that's clear enough. Get rid of information, before heading off to Chesters. It would suggest he was in the process of moving his operations prior to heading for the Roman fort. But we don't know why. Not yet. Of course, it might have some connection with Clifford's meeting in London, or maybe it was because of its cancellation? I've got a couple of men sifting through what papers remained, and doing some cross-checking but at this stage … who knows?'

'But you think it's all linked to Clifford's operation,' Grout suggested.

Cardinal grimaced. 'Maybe I'm just obsessed with nailing Clifford, tying everything into his operations. And Rigby was Clifford's man. So, I'm hoping so. I'm hoping we'll be able to find a connection between the murder of Rigby, and the whole business that Clifford's been running. So far, we can't be certain that this might be a gangland killing, or a personal matter, and to date we've no whisper from the Met that there is a link but then, they're not even sure that Clifford is still in their area. He seems to have gone to ground, while his other agents have also been scurrying for cover.'

'Sinking ship.'

Cardinal scowled. 'I don't think it'll be as good as that. No, the rats will be diving overboard because they've been told to do so. Yes, maybe Clifford's finding the heat too much for him; he might be wanting to close down some of his activities. But I have a feeling ...' He paused, reflectively.

'Sir?'

'I've just got a gut feeling something else is going down. Something we haven't yet thought about. Yes, it could just be my gut rumbling, but I feel Gus Clifford is just closing down temporarily because he's got some other iron he wants to heat up in the fire. But what that might be....'

Cardinal rose and walked across to the map on his wall. He stared at it moodily for a little while, then sighed, shook his head, turned back to Grout.

'Anyway, first thing is we have to get more information on these girls. If we're lucky, one of them will turn out to be the woman whom Gilbert met at The George. We need the answer to one question from her: was she waiting for Rigby or was she waiting for the man who killed him? And why did she go to ground so swiftly? What has she got to hide?'

That's three questions, Grout thought, not one. He did not say so.

'And then there's this photographer character, Paul Gilbert. I want a closer check done on him. I've been reading the notes on his interview and the statement he gave to the guys at Ponteland HQ. I'm not happy about them. As you said, it must have been clumsy, that inspector doesn't have the techniques.... Anyway, I think we need to have another chat with Mr Gilbert. We've got his address, he lives at Beverley, in the East Riding. I want you to take a car, Grout, and go pick him up. We'll use the York office to have a chat with him. I'll join you there this afternoon.'

Grout hesitated, opened his mouth, then closed it again. Cardinal scowled. He could guess what Grout was thinking.

'And since you're going to be near York, all right, I suppose we might as well let you indulge your passion for the academic – or is it the pornographic? You can do a detour, call in and go see this bookseller you're so keen to interview. When you find the time.' Cardinal shook his head disapprovingly. 'But I'll be more than surprised if Proud is of any use to us.'

Since his meeting with Cardinal was not due to take place until late afternoon, Grout decided to call on Philip Proud before he went out to Beverley to pick up Paul Gilbert. He left his car in the station car park and walked across the bridge and down past the Minster until he reached the Shambles. Proud's shop was just a short distance from St Hilary's and Grout found it immediately. He made no immediate attempt to enter; instead, he wandered along the Shambles for the sheer pleasure of taking in its mediaeval ambience. He found himself in agreement with the views of Professor Godfrey as he walked; Philip Proud's commercial venture was hardly in keeping with the nature of the street itself.

He turned, walked back from Clifford's Tower and returned to the bookshop. The narrow leaded windows of Philip Proud's enterprise were packed with paperbacks with sensational titles of the kind that would once have been seized by the police years earlier, as much for their failure to deliver what the covers promised, as much as anything else.

Grout entered the shop and found himself in a small room, the shelves being browsed among by several middle-aged gentlemen and a few prurient youngsters of school age. No one among the schoolboys seemed intent on buying; they were there for a thrill they were unlikely to achieve, and the boys should have been at school anyway, but Grout wasn't interested in doing anything about that. He made his way along towards the back of the room, glancing vacantly at some of the more lurid titles. Proud had spent a fair amount of money on his stock, that was clear enough. Much of it, in Grout's view, would have been wasted.

He became aware of someone standing behind him. He began to turn when the individual spoke quietly. 'This is all run of the mill stuff, of course. If you're at all interested, sir, we have some rather more fascinating material in the next room.'

Grout turned to stare at the young man who had addressed him. He guessed he was in his early twenties, and he was thin, dark-suited, sporting a pink shirt, floral tie and fashionably-framed spectacles. His hair was dark and neatly combed, and a hint of a moustache struggled for existence on his upper lip. His eyes were almost china-blue, and innocently frank. Grout supposed the projected innocence was one way of persuading the punters that all was on the level.

Grout nodded, saying nothing; the young man took it for acquiescence and gestured towards the back of the shop. He led the way. The room beyond was narrow and low-ceilinged; it was also rather dim. Grout stared at the shelves ranged around the room: there were books on flagellation, sadism, masochism, bondage, and a collection of Victorian bodice-rippers were grouped in one corner.

The young man turned, smiled with an affected shyness. 'Of course, if you're interested in something even more sophisticated—'

'I'm a police officer.'

'What? Oh, sod it!'

The two men stared at each other. The blue eyes had changed; the professional innocence was still there but now shadowed with chagrin and embarrassment. The young man seemed to regard Grout's presence as an unfair intrusion;

he was disturbed at his failure to recognize danger when it loomed up in front of him.

'I can usually spot the fuzz at a distance of half a mile,' he complained.

His tone was aggrieved. Grout shrugged. 'I'm not too happy myself, being taken for one of the dirty mac brigade.'

'Don't go any further,' the bookseller interrupted, holding up a warning hand. 'You know as well as I that there's nothing harmful in pornography and it's a mistake to classify all readers of erotica as sad, semi-deranged, hole in the corner, sexual fanatics. I like it myself, in fact,' he added rather gloomily. 'Sex, that is. I don't really go in for erotica.'

'You sell it,' Grout challenged.

'It's a way of making a living.'

'You're Philip Proud, I imagine.'

The blue eyes took on an expression of surprise. 'Yes, I am! How did you know my name? I don't use it in this business. *Fallacies Unlimited*. I would have used a different spelling but that would have appeared too in-your-face, and advertising might have been a problem. With objections from the rest of the Shambles, I would guess, too.' Philip Proud grimaced his dissatisfaction.

'And you deserted the academic world for this stuff.'

'That sounds like an echo from someone else I know.'

Grout glanced about him. It wasn't a good idea talking like this in the shop itself. 'Is there somewhere we can talk? Other than here. I don't imagine you want everyone to know you're being interviewed by a police officer. Bad for business, I would have thought.'

'And I suppose erotica makes you uncomfortable. I can understand that. But it's only a part of life.' Proud wrinkled his nose. 'But you're right. Some of my clients are easily embarrassed – even scared. I have a room upstairs that serves as an office. We can go there.'

Grout looked back to the room they were leaving. 'What about your present customers? Aren't you in danger of their stealing something if you're not around to watch?'

'I know most of them … apart from the kids. And they're not really purchasers, or thieves. They just like to stand there, read a while, dream, mentally masturbate…. Would you like to follow me?'

Proud led the way to a narrow staircase that took them to the upper floor. The office they entered was neat, and on the desk was a monitor that gave a view of the main room below and the front door. Proud was not as casual as he tried to make out; he could see what was going on downstairs while he was up here in the office.

'So,' Proud said as he perched one thigh on the edge of the desk, 'you from the vice squad, or what?'

'No. I've no interest in the tools of your trade.'

'No interest in erotica? So why are you here?' Proud asked.

'I'd like to talk to you about your thesis.'

There was a short, puzzled silence. 'My thesis? Why? It wasn't about sex in Rome or anything like that. I did include a few comments about some of the explicit statuary that was commonly held in respectable Roman homes, but there was nothing in it about erotomania or anything like that.'

'I told you, your selling of erotic literature – if that's what you call it – has no interest for me. I'm simply interested in why you deserted the academic life and—'

'Hold on! This'll be Professor Godfrey! He knows something about this. Nice chap, Godfrey, and he was very helpful to me when things got difficult. But he's somewhat narrowly-focussed. He got more than a bit stuffy about me opening this shop, felt I ought to have a crack at some academic posts, but teaching was never going to be my main aim in life. I'd had enough of it, the experience at university held bad vibes for me, this was a release into a world that erected a sort of buffer against those outside. My aunt of revered memory provided the means by popping her clogs after remembering me in her will. I set up the bookshop here, with that money. I don't make much of a living but I'm immersed, you know? Perhaps you might consider I'm hiding from my hidden psychological urges, my repressed desires or something, but who knows?'

'I'm no psychologist,' Grout admitted with a slight smile.

'No. Just a copper. I wonder what *your* hidden desires might be? You—'

'Never mind my hidden desires. Let's stick to the point. I understand that in your researches into mediaeval Italy you spent some time at Chesters Fort.'

There was a slight pause before Proud replied. 'That's so … though the two weren't really connected, except in a small way. But I don't—'

'Did you carry out any recording work in the storeroom there? Did you make a list of the holdings, for instance?'

Proud folded his arms and glared at Grout. Suddenly, his eyes were harder. 'What's this all about? Why are you harassing me?'

'*Harassing*? You think *this* is harassment? I've hardly started yet,' Grout admitted calmly.

'I don't see why I should go over my past life for you.'

'And I see no reason why I shouldn't swear out a warrant about some of the stuff you've got here,' Grout countered.

'It's not illegal!'

'I never said it was. But we could cause you trouble, looking just in case you were holding something … really nasty.

Paedophilia, for instance. Really dirty books.'

Proud held up his hands. 'All right, all right, let's not get touchy. You want answers. So just ask the questions.'

Grout smiled thinly. 'Good. So I'll ask you again. Did you make a list of the items in the Chesters storeroom when you worked there?'

Proud shrugged. 'I did. Well, to a certain extent. Items that interested me. But it was a while ago. I think I still have the list but I can't be sure. Let me think ...' He moved around the room, soft-footed, twisting his lip. He stood before a tall cupboard, opened the door and stared at the piles of folders, binders, and dusty account books. 'A lot of this is stuff already here, kept from the time when I took over. I've not dared touch it in case it all falls on my head. We need a woman's touch in this business. Fat chance, with my luck with women. But ... I have a feeling, a vague recollection that I might have stuffed the list up here, on the top shelf.' He glanced over his shoulder at Grout. 'I suppose you would have imagined I kept whips and leather stuff and dildos and other sex toys, that sort of thing here. Secreted away. But I'm a seller of books, not a practitioner. Just old files ...' Dust floated down upon him as he reached up to rummage in the documents on the top shelf. He drew some down, inspected them, shook his head. 'Wrong. Not here. But ... ah, of course!'

To one side of the cupboard was a wooden trunk of ancient vintage. He bent down and opened the lid.

'This was my grandfather's when he himself went to university,' Proud explained. 'I remember now, all the bits and pieces I had left when I left the university, I stuck it in here.'

'Your thesis?'

Proud shot a sharp glance in his direction. 'My thesis? No. But ... I guess you'll have already heard I lost it in a fire.'

'Professor Godfrey told me something about it. Yes. How

did that happen?'

'Long story.'

Grout sighed. 'That's what the Professor said. But he gave me a short version.'

Philip Proud pondered for a few moments. Then he grimaced. 'I don't know whether he ever believed my story. But no matter, he'd seen my work, supervised the writing while I was doing the research and he made out a case in my favour with the Senate. If it hadn't been for him, I wouldn't have been awarded my MA.'

Grout glanced down the main room of the bookshop. 'Not that you need it here.'

'You'd be surprised, my academic achievements provide a veneer of respectability for some of my customers. Persuades them they're not really kinky, to think of their bookseller as someone with a respectable academic background, a Masters degree no less.'

'I can see that. But let's get back to the loss of your thesis. Professor Godfrey said you claimed it was the result of vandalism by a bunch of students.'

Proud was leaning over the trunk and busily foraging inside its recesses. 'Something like that. Well, not exactly. You see, I was going out with this girl at the time. Pretty steady, really. I spent that particular evening at her flat, a rather crummy place on West Road, and I got back in the early hours to find my place had been ransacked.'

'Did you suspect it was a burglary?'

Proud glanced at him, shrugged. 'Maybe. But I had a theory ... You see, this girl I was dating, she'd been hitched up with this other guy for two years before she threw him over and started going out with me. He wasn't pleased, and when I got back to the flat and found the place had been turned over and my thesis destroyed, well, I thought of him straightaway. My laptop had gone as well, so I thought if I went straight over to his place and confronted him maybe I'd get the laptop back at least. So I charged over there, two in the morning, hammered on his door, we had a right old barney but he denied everything ... and there was no laptop. Anyway, I still suspected he had a hand in the business, but now, I'm not so sure ...'

'The girl?'

'He married her a year later. *C'est la vie*. Hey, here we are. The very thing you're looking for, though God knows why! *Voila*! The storeroom list. I wonder why I ever bothered to keep it.'

Proud had drawn from the depths of the trunk a faded notebook which he flourished under Grout's nose. Grout took it from him and inspected a few pages.

'It appears to be just a lot of scribbled notes.'

Proud stretched and yawned prodigiously, then scratched at his nose as though annoyed by dust arising from the trunk. 'Yeah, well, I think you'll find what you seem to be looking for towards the back. The notes are some of the preparation stuff I did for my thesis. In the end that was about all that was left after the thesis and the laptop disappeared. There was some other information I kept for a while but after I got the MA award confirmed I threw it out. Don't know why I kept that notebook in fact. Overlooked it, I guess. Anyway, is that what you want?'

Grout checked the last few pages of the book, and nodded. 'May I take it away with me?'

'Hang it on your wall for all I care. It's yesterday's news as far as I'm concerned.' Proud eyed Grout for a moment then allowed a mischievous smile to touch his lips. 'But like I said before, there's far more interesting stuff in the back room, if you have that sort of inclination....'

With the notebook safely stowed in the glove compartment of his car, Grout took the road to Beverley. He had little difficulty finding Paul Gilbert's house, it was a large, rambling, Victorian building, probably a former vicarage, standing on a corner where three lanes met and it commanded a pleasant view of the countryside around the town. Whether Gilbert made a good living from his photography Grout had no idea, but it was clear that the man lived in a certain style. The house was expensive, in a sought after area. The car wheels rasped over a gravelled drive as Grout drove up to the front door. The garage stood to one side of the house; its doors were open and the garage itself empty.

Grout parked, got out, locked the car and made his way up to the front door. He rang the ornately framed bell. He could hear the sound echoing within the house but no one came to the door. He tried again but there was still no reply. It seemed the house, as well as the garage, was unoccupied. Gilbert was not at home.

Grout waited, considering. He could go back to the office or he could wait here a-while in case Gilbert turned up. He checked his watch and decided he would wait a little while, rather than return to York. He used his mobile to ring in to the office in York and left a message there for Cardinal, explaining he was waiting. A few minutes later he received a text message to say that the chief inspector had gone to Sheffield.

He sat on a bench in the front garden for an hour, enjoying the pale sunshine, and casually flicked through the pages of the notebook Philip Proud had given him He saw nothing there that might have been important. He wondered what Cardinal was up to.

*

James Cardinal had been met at Sheffield railway station by a police car. He had decided to go there from Newcastle after receiving a phone call from the Sheffield CID.

The car took him swiftly away from the city centre and along the Glossop Road. It went past two sets of traffic lights, turned right, and slowed as it approached a street of houses that had been built perhaps eighty years earlier but which had now been turned into self-contained apartments, one up, one down. The gardens in front of the houses were in various states of disuse. There were already two police cars parked outside one of the houses, towards the end of a *cul de sac*. A small group of people stood to one side, craning for a view, gossiping, and there was a ripple of excitement as Cardinal's car arrived. As far as he could see, no journalists so far. That at least was a bonus, he thought sourly. Cardinal got out of the car, ignored the throng and entered the house where a uniformed policeman was standing impassively on guard. As he entered the corridor leading to the downstairs flat, he was met by an officer of the same rank as himself.

'Where is she?' Cardinal asked, dispensing with any ceremony.

The Sheffield officer directed him towards the bedroom. The body awaited his inspection.

She lay on her back, half on and half off the bed. Her arms were thrown back across the rumpled coverlet and her knees had buckled where she had slid downwards in the struggle. Death had not been kind to her, it had ripped away her beauty. Her hair had been torn out at one side of her head and the bare patch was stained with coagulated blood. The skin along her jaw line had been scratched as though a sharp instrument had scored its way across her skin, possibly a ring. But it was the belt that had killed her. It was a cheap plastic belt, black in colour, shiny, an accessory Cardinal assumed might have been used on a woman's dress. But this belt had bitten cruelly into the woman's throat, effectively cutting off air to her lungs. As she had been strangled to death her tongue had forced its way out between her teeth, and there was a trickle of blood on her left cheek where those teeth had clamped down in agony on her tongue.

'Do we know who she was?' Cardinal asked.

The officer at his shoulder looked at him. 'My name's Carlton. Chief Inspector. You're DCI Cardinal, I gather.'

When Cardinal glared at him Carlton raised his chin. 'Nice to know who one is talking to, no?' His voice was clipped, educated, no trace of a Yorkshire accent. 'Yes, we think we know her identity. Her name is … was … Eloise Parker, it seems. There's evidence she used other aliases, in addition. I'm told she was a photographic model, whatever that means, though it might well have been a cover for a whole host of activities as we all know. There's some evidence she was legitimate, though how successful, one doesn't know.'

'Doesn't one?' Cardinal could not resist asking.

Carlton raised a dismissive eyebrow but did not rise to the bait. 'We've found a list of her contacts in the modelling world. It includes some reputable people. There's a scrapbook too, with some shots of her that were taken a few years ago. Not very much that's recent, so maybe she's been on the slide for a while. That, or there's the possibility she's been concentrating on other activities. What exactly, I wouldn't know, but one can hazard a guess…. Modelling and entertaining clients, we've seen the slide happen often enough, haven't we? But I was advised to call you….' There was an edge of hostility creeping into his tone. 'Call you, because she answers the description put out from Morpeth. The Northumberland police told me you'd be interested in this one. As far as I'm concerned, you can have it if you like. Never did like dealing with murder inquiries.'

Cardinal decided to capitulate to some extent, he was off his regular patch in any case. He took out a cigarette case, extracted a cigarette and offered one to Carlton. He rarely smoked these days, and even more rarely on duty, but there was a bitter taste in his mouth. He was hoping he could have questioned this girl. She wouldn't be able to tell him anything about events at The George Hotel now.

'This girl ... Parker, you say? So she checked into The George Hotel under an assumed name... I gather you found some connection with the dead man, Rigby.'

Carlton had refused the offer of a cigarette and was staring coldly at the one that remained unlit between Cardinal's fingers. 'This is a crime scene. I don't think it's a good idea if you smoke.'

'Of course. Sorry.' Cardinal returned the cigarette to its silver case.

'Yeah, we found a link. There's a bunch of letters in the bureau, unpaid bills, usual stuff ... but there's one or two items which suggest Rigby is the man who was paying the rent on this flat. We'll check further, of course, but it looks like Rigby had set her up here. For obvious reasons, one would guess. All fairly recent, though.'

Cardinal took a deep breath. He nodded. 'And how long has she been dead?'

'The signs are it happened some time yesterday, but you know what forensics are like: they'll never give you a straight answer until they've gone through everything and thought it over. So, no precise time, but maybe early last night.' He hesitated, chewed at his lip. 'We do have a few other leads to follow up, even so.'

'Such as?'

The Sheffield CID man stroked his chin thoughtfully, and grimaced. 'Well, we know she was getting ready to go out somewhere when her visitor called. According to her diary, she had two appointments set up by a modelling agency. When we contacted them they told us she had cancelled the appointments, told them she'd be out of touch for a while. One of the staff at the agency told me early this afternoon that enquiries were being made about her and an address was given out, but for some reason no record was kept of the caller ... it was done by phone. Slapdash, when you think about it. After all, how can the agency keep tabs and earn its money?'

'Anything else?' Cardinal asked.

Carlton grunted. 'We've got the usual standby, a nosy neighbour. Surprising really, you'd think in flats like these people no longer have time to skulk behind curtains and watch what's going on. But the old lady across the way ... she's about seventy but still has her wits about her ... she says there was a car parked in the street for quite a while yesterday evening. Not a locally owned car, she knew all those, she reckoned. The vehicle was driven away about eight, returned again at ten for about an hour, and then went off again. She didn't see who was driving it. But she heard some odd noises in the street about midnight, she got up and took a look outside and saw that the car was back. As far she could make out, anyway, because it was dark. And she wasn't really sure about the time.'

'Bit imprecise.'

'You said it.'

'Was it she who put out the alarm call?'

'Found the body, you mean? As a matter of fact, it was. No one else in the street seems to have noticed, but when she was up and about, our neighbour saw the front door to the downstairs flat was ajar. She was on her way out herself, to visit the mini-market down the road. Anyway, she nosed inside, called out to Miss Parker, and when she got no answer she took a look around.'

'Public-spirited citizen.'

'Nosy old fanny, you mean. Still, she got the shock she deserved. Let out a scream, scuttled outside, back to her own house, rang 999. And that's when the cavalry arrived.'

'This old lady, she couldn't say what car it was she saw? Registration, that sort of thing.'

Carlton shook his head. 'You'd have thought not, wouldn't you? She couldn't give us a number, though she thinks it might have had a 6 in it … which is little help. But make of the car, that's another thing. She reckoned it was a Ford Focus. How about that? You'd think an old girl like that wouldn't be interested in cars. But she regularly takes the Auto Trader apparently, even though she's not in the market to buy.'

'Misspent youth, perhaps?'

Carlton managed a smile. 'Back seat in inexpensive cars, you mean? Could be. But, there you are. I have to say, I don't take to the old girl much, but at least I can say we could do with eyes like hers among some of the coppers I have to work with.'

CHAPTER SIX

G ROUT WAS BORED and frustrated. There had been no sign
of his quarry. He felt he was wasting his time hanging
around the house but Cardinal had been specific in his instructions and Grout knew better than to cross the old man. Not
that he would get any Brownie points for hanging around, he
had the feeling that he'd get bawled out whichever decision he
took. Cardinal didn't like to be kept waiting, he expected that
matters would be followed through with expedition. Even if
delay was due to no fault of Grout's.

He checked his watch, and decided he'd give it another half
hour. No sooner had he made the decision than he realized it
wasn't necessary. He caught a glimpse in his rear mirror of a car
turning into the drive. He waited a few minutes, then started
his engine, edged his own car forward until it was half-hidden
behind a screen of trees but in such a position that the driver of
the car coming up to the house would not see him immediately.
He watched as the car nosed towards the garage. The driver
killed the engine, got out of the car, locked the door and began
to walk towards the house when he caught sight of Grout's
vehicle.

He froze.

Grout had the feeling that the man was poised, contemplating flight. It would take little to send him irrationally leaping for his car. He waited. Then after a moment the man's shoulders slumped. Grout breathed a relieved sigh and got out of the car, he had no appetite for a wild chase in the countryside.

'Mr Gilbert?'

Paul Gilbert leaned back against the bonnet of his vehicle, folded his arms and affected a casual pose as Grout walked towards him. Then, suddenly, unexpectedly, the man doubled up, bent forward, clutching his hands to his stomach. The sounds were unmistakeable, he retched, vomited in what seemed a panicked reaction. Grout hesitated, slowed, walked forward carefully.

'Are you all right?'

There was no reply apart from a continuation of the violent retching. But as Grout stood there, slowly the pained sounds ceased, drily.

Gilbert brought out a handkerchief and wiped his mouth and face. He stepped aside from the pool of vomit on the drive. He was sweating profusely; Grout noted the perspiration glistening on his face. He avoided Grout's glance.

'I'm sorry ... I'm not feeling well.' Gilbert's voice was muffled by the handkerchief.

Grout thought it was quite understandable. Even from where he stood some feet away from the man he had come to interview, the stench of regurgitated whiskey was palpable. Gilbert had clearly been hitting the bottle hard, even this early in the day.

'We'd better go inside,' Grout suggested, extending a reluctant helping hand.

Gilbert ignored the assistance and lurched towards the front door of the house. He had some difficulty locating the appropriate key from the ring. Grout waited patiently then followed Gilbert into the house as he switched on the lights inside the entrance hall.

'I need a drink.'

Grout thought that was perhaps the last thing Gilbert needed but made no demur, it was neither his house nor his stomach. They entered the sitting room. Gilbert staggered towards a drinks cabinet, clutching his stomach, then poured himself a stiff scotch, making no offer to his visitor. Grout watched impassively as Gilbert collapsed on the brocade settee without removing his coat. Grout looked around him.

It was an expensively furnished room with deep comfortable chairs, a piano, stereophonic recording equipment and a series of elegantly framed photographs adorning the expensively papered walls. Several of the photographs were of carefully posed girls, young, nubile, scantily clothed, with the usual parted, expectant lips, awaiting breathlessly the inspection of the viewer. He guessed they were examples of Gilbert's own work. The man did not seem to Grout to be the kind of individual who would be inclined to show the work of others.

Grout looked back at the man sprawled on the settee. Gilbert's eyes were closed, his fingers loosely gripping the saviour whiskey, the beverage intended to replace what he had already lost in the driveway. There was no doubt in Grout's mind that there would be no problem hauling Gilbert in right now, for being intoxicated in charge of a car. But there would be little point to that, it would be better to have a quiet chat with Gilbert in his own house, and see what transpired.

'Do you remember me, Mr Gilbert?' he asked quietly.

It required a certain effort on the part of the eminent photographer to open his eyes. Further effort led to his raising his head to blink, focus weakly, and then nod. 'You're that copper.

You were at The George ... I was questioned ... what the hell are you doing here?'

'You've a good memory, Mr Gilbert, on even a short acquaintance. But why am I here? Just to ask a few more questions. Regarding your memory for a start ... was yours really that good, when we spoke that day at The George Hotel?'

'What you talking about?' Gilbert said peevishly.

He seemed in no mood to answer. His head dropped, he struggled to a more upright position and he began to retch again. The glass of whisky was spilled. Grout stepped back, looked about him, saw the half-open door across the room and wondered whether it was a bathroom. Gilbert needed a glass of water, not more alcohol. But when he looked through the door, he realized it was a small room that Gilbert had clearly furnished as a work room of sorts, for mounting and framing prints. It was cluttered with photographic material and equipment with some unmounted shots being some three or four feet across, but Grout suspected this was not Gilbert's main studio. That would be elsewhere, away from such clutter. Then his attention was caught by one particular unframed blow-up that occupied a position of prominence in the room.

It was the photograph of a woman, walking along a terrace beside a river, with a stone bridge in the background.

It took only moments for Grout to recognize the setting; the features of the woman were somewhat indistinct since she was looking away, but he could see that the shot had been taken in the gardens of The George Hotel at Chollerford.

He stared at it thoughtfully for a little while, then turned and went back into the sitting room. Gilbert was sitting up, staring vacantly at the empty glass spilled on the rug in front of him. He seemed unhappy and depressed. Grout stood in front of him, waiting.

At last Gilbert looked up at him, eyes vacant.

Grout leaned forward. 'When you were questioned at The George Hotel, your answers seemed to me to be somewhat vague. But they interested me.'

'Is that so?' The words were belligerent, careless, the tone defeated.

'The information you gave was somewhat precise.'

'What the hell you talking about? Isn't that a good thing?' Gilbert asked wearily. He stared unhappily at the stains on the rug before him.

'You answered with precision. Very, sort of, strict answers to questions. And you didn't exactly lie, did you? Perhaps … just left things out, is that right?'

Gilbert made no immediate reply, but now a certain evasiveness had crept into his glance. An edgy atmosphere seemed to be building up between the two men and it was sobering Gilbert quickly. Soon he would forget he was feeling ill.

'For instance,' Grout murmured almost casually, 'with respect to the woman you met, you said you didn't go into her room with her. The inspector who questioned you, he put a certain interpretation on that … but another occurred to me. You might have meant you didn't go to the room *with* her, but that wouldn't preclude you from having visited her later on, would it?'

Gilbert opened his mouth as though about to reply, but then thought better of it and remained silent.

'And again,' Grout suggested, 'you said she gave you her name and that was all. Perhaps my ears are unduly sensitive but it seemed to me that there was a current of resentment in your tone when you made that statement. I wondered what that might be … so, what exactly were you trying to tell us in that statement, Mr Gilbert?'

Gilbert hesitated, then shook his head. 'I don't know what you're on about. I've nothing to add to what I said at the time. I don't know what you're trying to imply. I never stepped inside that room of hers. I never touched her, never seduced her. I didn't really know her or anything about her. There was a bit of a chat, a drink, and then, after that, we went our separate ways. That's all there was to it. I haven't seen her, or heard from her since.'

'But you took her photograph. I've just seen it in your processing room.'

Gilbert hesitated, glanced furtively to the room in question. 'Well, I ...' He seemed to be about to make some sort of denial but realized it would be a waste of time. His shoulders slumped and he was suddenly very pale. Grout smiled at him but there was no warmth in the smile.

'When you were interviewed you specifically stated you had not taken any shots of the woman. But in fact you had. So why didn't you see fit to mention the photographs to the police? What were you trying to hide? Not just the photographs, I guess.'

'I wasn't asked about it,' Gilbert replied in a surly tone.

'Oh, come off it, Gilbert. I know you denied it. Besides, you knew we were trying to trace this girl. We had a description but that was all we had to go on. You must have realized that a photograph would have been invaluable to us. And you didn't even mention it? In fact, you denied taking any! Why? What were you trying to hide?'

'Hide? Nothing!' Gilbert licked dry lips, and he leaned forward, seizing his knees fiercely. He shook his head as though trying to escape a sudden dizziness. 'Not telling you ... I wasn't asked ... I didn't hide anything ... I did nothing wrong!'

'On the contrary. You lied to us. You took a photograph

of the girl; you knew we were looking for her; you withheld the photograph. This behaviour of yours, lying to the police, hiding evidence of her identity, it could lead to a degree of unpleasantness and harassment, Gilbert, believe me. Trouble could be heading your way.'

'No!' Gilbert's tone was strangled and he stared at Grout in a desperation that was surprising. 'Look, I told you, I did nothing wrong! I wasn't withholding the shot deliberately, I mean, I had no intention of misleading anyone. But can't you understand? I didn't mention it because I just didn't want to get *involved.*'

'You'll have to explain that to me rather more fully,' Grout said coldly.

'I didn't want to get involved. All that police activity, finding the body at Chesters, I was shocked, I wasn't thinking straight. And the girl ...'

'Yes?'

Gilbert heaved a despondent, defeated sigh. 'All right, I admit I was interested in her. It's true I bought her a drink; I chatted her up. I thought I was in with a chance, if you know what I mean. I tried to get off with her. And I got the impression she was leading me on. We walked on the terrace, I kissed her ... and then she agreed that I should go to her room after a short interval. But ...' Gilbert looked at Grout with a sudden, sullen defiance. 'But when I went there, the bitch had locked the door. She had me standing there, almost pleading. And she stayed silent.'

'She was in the room?'

'I'm pretty certain of that. She was just playing a game, wasn't she? Turning me on, then hanging me out to dry. Humiliating me.... And in the morning ... she was gone. I didn't see her again.'

'You could have told us all this earlier,' Grout growled.

'What difference would it have made? I just explained to you, I didn't want to be involved in all this mess. I didn't want to admit she'd made a fool of me … getting me interested, and then locking the bloody door!'

'And you're certain she was inside the room.'

Miserably, Gilbert shrugged. 'I *thought* she was. At the time, I was certain she was. But now, thinking back, after I'd returned to my own room, and I was lying there frustrated, alone on my bed, I heard a car leave The George Hotel car park. Maybe she had already decided to leave the hotel; maybe that was her car. Or maybe someone else's. I don't know. The headlights flashed over my room ceiling. I remember thinking …'

He fell silent.

Grout's tone was cold. 'It would have been better if you'd told us all this earlier. It could have made things easier for us. As it is, I think you'd better come with me to headquarters at York where you can make a statement—'

'Oh, there's no need for that,' boomed a voice from the open doorway. 'We can just continue the interview right here.'

Cardinal smiled almost affably as he settled himself into a chair and stretched out his long legs. He sighed. He looked at the two surprised individuals facing him. 'That's better. Car seats do my back no good. I hope you don't mind, Mr Gilbert, my appearing unannounced like this. The front door was open. I saw my colleague's car. My name's Cardinal, by the way. Detective Chief Inspector. You'd have expected Grout to make the necessary introductions, wouldn't you? But there you are….'

Grout glared at the senior officer. Affability was a quality he had not come across in Cardinal before but there seemed to be a great deal of it in evidence now. It made him suspicious.

'I didn't realize—' he began but Cardinal waved him to silence with an expansive gesture.

'Don't worry about it, Grout. Bad manners, in my experience, is a general failing in the young and inexperienced. Social courtesies get left by the way. And I know you and I were supposed to meet at headquarters, but I got tied up in other enquiries, couldn't have made it so when I got the message from you that you were still waiting to interview Mr Gilbert, I thought I'd meet you here.'

He smiled at the pale-faced man on the settee.

'And you'll be Mr Gilbert, of course. I'm sure you'll agree it's far more cosy to have a routine chat here, isn't it, rather than at headquarters?'

Grout continued to stare at Cardinal, who had folded his arms, crossed his feet at the ankles and assumed the expression of a benign uncle.

'Now, Mr Gilbert, you were explaining something to young Grout here.'

After a brief hesitation Gilbert repeated what he had said to Grout, a little warily, but he seemed to relax somewhat as Cardinal frowned in understanding and nodded his head sagely.

'Well, I can see how you felt, not least after the unpleasant experience of stumbling over a corpse on your morning stroll. Still, better late than never, hey? And as for giving us information about the woman, well, I mean, I know you have a reputation to maintain and as a photographer you wouldn't want to have your name closely linked with this unfortunate, and rather mysterious young woman, would you? But of course we would like to have a copy of the photograph—'

'There's a big one in the room over there,' Grout snapped irritably.

Cardinal eyed him coolly as Gilbert babbled his assurance, rose and almost scurried into the other room.

'Yes, of course, you can take the print.'

He seemed relieved by Cardinal's relaxed manner. Grout glowered, wondering what had brought about his senior's easiness; Chief Inspector Cardinal was normally renowned for his short temper and gracelessness with colleagues. And he had said something about the woman … Grout was unable to pursue it for the moment.

'How long have you been in the photography business?' Cardinal asked when Gilbert hurried back from the other room with the print in his hands.

'Twelve years, now.' Gilbert was sufficiently relieved even to indulge in a little boasting. 'In that time, I've made quite a reputation in certain circles—'

'And written a few books.'

'Well, they're really photographic essays,' Gilbert replied smugly. 'Shall I get some backing for this print or will you just roll it—'

'I suppose this line of work takes you about the country a fair bit,' Cardinal interrupted.

Gilbert shrugged. 'Certainly around the northern counties. I've tended to restrict my work to Lancashire, Durham, and Cumbria, both for aesthetic reasons and as a way of staying away from some of those sharks down south. I tell you, it's criminal what they charge for gallery displays—'

'Very interesting.' Cardinal cut him short and turned to Grout. 'By the way, I've had some further information about Gus Clifford. He was seen in London yesterday afternoon, so he's not away yet. And we've also arranged to get details of the fencing arrangements in place for some of the art thefts last year. It would seem the pieces in question, which we are certain Clifford was involved with, were moved out to Switzerland to a receiver who was the director of a registered auction company in Basel. Each picture was catalogued then sold on to a member of the ring. Each 'sale' gave the picture provenance, a spurious legal coverage so that when it was passed on to a private buyer – not in open auction, of course – he'd have some paperwork to cover his back in due course. The buyers are probably up to the whole fiddle, up to their necks no doubt, but that's where we've got so far.'

Cardinal smiled. Grout stared at him, astonished that Cardinal would be speaking so freely in front of Paul Gilbert. Then Cardinal turned to the photographer. 'You've heard of Clifford, I suppose?'

Gilbert's features displayed only polite interest.

'Clifford? Is he a dealer?'

'I suppose you could call him that,' Cardinal said and laughed.

'I'm not sure … I can't really place the name among the people I've been dealing with over the years.'

'No matter. But these trips of yours, when you traipse around photographing things, I suppose you keep a record of them?'

'Naturally, since I have expenses to note for my accounts, and believe me, I have a meticulous accountant. And I need the records for the shots, of course, to use them as the basis of captions I'll use later in my publications. You can forget so easily, when you're moving around. So I have records of dates, places, atmospheric conditions, lens focal number, exposure time, all the professional data that one needs to maintain to—'

'Yes, I'm sure. But it's just the places you've visited that I'm interested in.' Cardinal's tone was still affable and relaxed as he smiled benignly at Gilbert. 'So, let's test your memory. Let's take a random date. Let's say 9th March last year.'

'Ninth of March.' Gilbert screwed up his eyes in thought. 'Not easy … March … hold on, yes, that's when I would've been working the border castles. I was somewhere around Berwick round about that date. I was working my way gradually south.'

Cardinal seemed genuinely pleased. 'Very good! So let's try another. February this year?'

Gilbert nodded, at ease now. 'Beginning of the month, that's easy. I was in Leeds. After that, I moved up to Durham but for details I'd have to consult my diary of course, my working diary, that is—'

'Odd, really.' Some of the relaxed ease was leaching from Cardinal's manner and Grout detected a certain edge of steel entering his tone. 'It's interesting, but on 9th March last year there happened to have been a theft of jewellery from the Delavere mansion in Northumberland. Not too far from Berwick, yes? And in February of this year an auction room in Sunderland was raided and some valuable silver stolen. You were in Durham, you say?'

'I don't see …' The immediate protestation on Gilbert's lips died. His eyes widened, and he stared at Cardinal as though he was looking at a particularly poisonous snake. 'You're hardly suggesting … Northumberland is a big county.'

'So is Durham,' Cardinal replied flatly. 'Equally, a job that takes you around the counties regularly can be a good cover for nefarious activity such as the looting of auction rooms … or being on hand to accept stuff and dispose of it according to instructions. And you say you've never heard of Gus Clifford?'

Gilbert shook his head angrily. 'You must be mad! You can't be suggesting—'

'I'm not suggesting anything yet, Mr Gilbert. I'm just asking questions. I'm simply pointing out a few facts to you. Now let's add to them. You stayed at the same hotel as a woman who was probably tied in with a member of a gang of thieves. A man by the name of Rigby. I don't suppose you know him, either, hey? You were seen with this woman, spoke to her, took her photograph – with or without her permission – and tried to seduce her about the time her boyfriend got his skull crushed. Before, or maybe after, you were failing miserably to get what you wanted. But we don't really have a timeline on all this, do we? Did the events coincide? Or did one follow on from the other?'

Gilbert bobbed up in his seat. Indignation scored his features, alarm squeaked in his voice. 'But what you're saying, what you're implying, it's all wrong! It's twisted! It wasn't like that. I never saw the dead man before I found him up at the bath house. And the girl, I was just—'

'You were just what?' Cardinal sneered. 'Just trying to make time with her behind her boyfriend's back?'

'I'm telling you I didn't even know her, never met her before that night. I didn't know the man up at Chesters, and I didn't know he was linked to her. As for all this rubbish about thefts in the northern counties, I can't see what it's got to do with me.'

Cardinal silenced his tirade with a sharp gesture. He rose from his chair and advanced menacingly upon Gilbert. 'Don't play games with me, Gilbert,' he snarled, injecting venom into his tone. 'You've already held up our investigations by with-holding evidence.'

'I swear to you I never saw that woman before that night!'

'But you wanted to see her again, isn't that right?'

Something again kicked in with Grout. Cardinal had earlier spoken of the woman as mysterious, and *unfortunate*. He looked at the detective chief inspector and then glanced at Gilbert. The man's features were covered in a light sheen of sweat. He stared at Cardinal with the eyes of a dog that had been unjustly kicked.

'What car do you drive?' Cardinal asked quietly.

'It's ... it's a Ford Focus.'

'Colour?'

'Light green. What—'

'Is that the car outside the garage?' Cardinal interrupted him.

Gilbert licked dry lips. He nodded, scared. 'Yes, that's the one. Why do you ask?'

Cardinal grimaced, stared at him silently for several seconds then turned away and glanced at Grout.

'We found the woman.'

Grout made no reply. He was watching Gilbert. Plain terror now glared out of the man's eyes as he riveted his attention on Cardinal's back.

'I received a call from the Sheffield police,' Cardinal explained coldly. 'They'd been presented with a corpse answering the description we put out. Her real name's Eloise Parker. Or was. So we won't really need Mr Gilbert's photograph of her now, not for identification purposes, at least. Miss Parker has been strangled. Attractive she might have been, but she's not pretty any longer.' He looked at Gilbert, scowled. 'Maybe you'd like to take another photograph for your album. Sort of before and after, if you know what I mean.'

'That's sick,' Gilbert croaked.

'Don't like 'em dead, do you?' Cardinal's mouth twisted unpleasantly. He observed the man carefully for a little while, noting the stains of vomit on his clothing. 'Were you hitting the bottle hard last night?'

Gilbert made no reply.

'Perhaps you'd like to tell me, Mr Gilbert, what precisely you were doing yesterday and the day before? Working? Or checking on photographic agencies?'

'Why would I want to do that?'

'Because the woman you met at The George Hotel worked as a model. My feeling is you knew that ... or guessed it.'

Gilbert shivered. 'I want to see my solicitor,' he whispered.

'That's your privilege,' Cardinal grunted, unmoved. Gilbert nevertheless seemed incapable of movement, so he went on, 'Someone's been checking up on the dead woman ... we know that from the agencies. A neighbour saw a car outside her place. Was it your car, Gilbert?' When Gilbert still made no reply, Cardinal suddenly snapped, 'Was it because she still wouldn't have you that you killed her?'

Gilbert leaped to his feet, stood there swaying unsteadily. He was shuddering and his eyes were wild. He glared at Cardinal, then at Grout and seemed to lose control. 'You're crazy! You can't believe that! I don't know what you're talking about! I was never—'

'A light green Ford Focus was seen parked near the flat where the dead girl was found. It was your car, Gilbert – admit it! Come on, you've left a trail any fool can follow. First you withhold information, fail to help identify the woman, then you check with the agencies, find her address and go parking outside her flat! If it wasn't your fingers who tightened the belt that throttled the life out of her—'

The last vestiges of resistance crumbled in Paul Gilbert. He glanced wildly about him, as though he felt himself trapped. 'This is madness! I ... I never ... my car... All right, all right, I admit I went there, but I didn't ... I never *touched* her. She was dead before I even got into the flat.' He stopped suddenly, moaned. 'I want to phone my solicitor....'

Cardinal's tone was suddenly gentler. 'All right, my friend, you can talk to your solicitor. Use your mobile or the house phone. But before you do, off the record, you might like to tell us your side of this story. What do you have to lose? If your story checks out we can let you just fade from the scene. No more hassle. So what do you say?'

Gilbert grabbed eagerly at the opportunity. The story was quickly, if incoherently, related. Grout listened while Gilbert gabbled his tale to Cardinal, and recognized the bottled-up tension in the man, the sexual frustration, the blow to his pride by the rejection he had suffered at Chesters. Gilbert was a womaniser; there was no telling what degree of success he was accustomed to obtaining but it was certain that his failure with Eloise Parker had hit him hard. It had built up a determination to seek her out, find her, persuade her into a closer relationship with him. What he had to say largely confirmed what Cardinal had already suggested.

It had not been too difficult, Gilbert explained, finding her. He had noted a certain grace, a way of carrying herself that had suggested to his experienced eye that she had worked as a professional model. He had his own shot of the girl so he had simply checked with the photographic agencies known to him, narrowed the search down to five firms and had been given access to their files in view of his own recognized status as a photographer. He had wheedled the information out of the last agency, learned her name and obtained her address, even though it seemed she had somewhat faded from the modelling scene of recent months. She lived in Sheffield. He had gone there.

'The flat was rented by Joseph Rigby, the man whose body you found,' Cardinal said coldly.

'I knew nothing about that.' Gilbert's immediate reaction

changed and his eyes widened. 'Rigby … you say that was the man I found up at Chesters, but how was I to know his identity?'

'The dead man was the woman's lover.'

'I didn't know that. How could I? I didn't know who she was, didn't know she was tied up with this man when I met her. How the hell could I? I only met her for the first time at The George Hotel that night!'

'But how did you expect to press your suit,' Grout asked, 'by going round to her place in Sheffield?'

'Press his *suit*?' Cardinal asked, wonderingly. Grout was certainly of the old school, in spite of his age. Grout shot an irritated glance in his direction.

'I'd got her photograph,' Gilbert babbled. 'I just thought … if I went there and told her I'd kept it from the police, how I was looking after her, keeping her out of trouble, well, she might be … grateful, me helping her escape the attention of the police.'

'But not escaping *your* attentions,' Grout murmured. Cardinal was still staring at him, clearly amazed by Grout's choice of words. Gilbert rubbed his mouth with the back of his hand.

'So, Mr Gilbert, what happened when you got there?' Cardinal asked.

'I … I went to the address. She wasn't in. I parked, waited in the street for a few hours. I wanted to see her,' he said miserably. 'I must have been crazy. But after what happened … or really, didn't happen – at Chesters … at the hotel she was just another woman. But later … I couldn't forget her. It was like I was on fire. Couldn't keep still. Couldn't get her out of my mind.'

'So you waited in the street,' Cardinal said, prodding to get him on with his story, rather than wallow in his frustrated misery.

121

'I left to get something to eat about eight, I hadn't eaten all day. Then I came back, waited, left to get some petrol before the station closed, came back and it was only then that I tried her door again. This time … it was unlocked. I went in. I called out.' He took a gulp of air. 'I called … and then I saw her.'

'What time was this?'

Gilbert shrugged, shook his head. 'I can't be certain. About 12.30 I guess. Maybe a bit later. I don't know. I was in shock.'

'Why didn't you report her death to the police?' Cardinal asked.

Gilbert hesitated. 'I was in shock, I just told you! I got out of there fast, like a bat out of hell. But I did *think* of calling in. I took out my mobile phone, was about to make a report, then realized if I made the call it could be traced later even if I didn't leave my name … and I didn't want to be involved. Too many questions. Too much hassle. Too much explaining to do. So I never made the call. I kept my head down. I drove home.'

He shivered as though someone was walking over his grave.

'When I got home I couldn't sleep. I took a few drinks, but it didn't help. I lay awake all night, absolutely terrified. I didn't feel I could go to the police, couldn't explain about her, about the photographs, finding her dead. I was afraid …'

'You've made things a damn sight worse for yourself,' Cardinal growled, 'and impeded our investigations. Couldn't you see delay would make your story more difficult to believe?'

'Look, I swear I didn't kill her! I didn't even *touch* her when I found her. I wanted her, I lusted after her, couldn't get her out of my mind. Now I can't get the memory of her just lying there, different, horrible … I can't eat. I can't sleep, I've been drinking, I went out to a pub, and when I got back here tonight and saw a strange car in the drive the panic just overwhelmed me. I've been sick as a dog …'

After Gilbert had been taken out to the squad car that Cardinal had called in, to be taken to York to make a complete statement, Cardinal joined Grout as he gathered up piles of photographs recently taken by the photographer on his expeditions. He watched him push a thick wad of prints on Chesters Fort into a file and tie it up with string.

'So, you reckon his story stands up?'

Grout tucked the file under his arm, looked down at the floor and shrugged. 'I don't know, sir. He's probably telling the truth, to my mind. But what about your remarks regarding the Clifford gang? Do we really have anything to back up the suggestion Gilbert was involved with Clifford?'

Cardinal grunted and shook his head 'Nothing, really. I was just testing the water, and trying to throw a scare into him. I wanted to see how he'd react. But we got nothing, really.' He sighed. 'Well, we'll get a team in to turn this place upside down, see what we find. But like you I get the feeling Gilbert has no link to Clifford … and probably no link to Rigby. He just stumbled upon the body.… It was all just coincidence.'

'You're ruling out the possibility this could have been a crime – the killing of the woman – that had nothing to do with Gilbert getting revenge, or letting his anger overcome him when he got rejected a second time?'

'You think he's the type?' Cardinal didn't wait for an answer. 'No, I think Gilbert's no strong-arm man. I think we need to look elsewhere for the woman's killer.'

'Clifford?'

'He's still around in the background, isn't he?'

'So how do you see it all, sir?' Grout asked carefully.

'I'm not sure yet.' Cardinal bit his lip, chewed at it thoughtfully. 'The evidence we've got so far makes a hazy picture but

I think I can see some possibilities emerging. I have the feeling maybe Rigby was wanting to get out of the organization, or possibly Clifford caught him with his fingers in the till on his own account, something along those lines. He didn't move fast enough and Clifford caught up with him. Gus Clifford was either up at Chesters himself, or sent one of his thugs, or even a contracted killer, and Rigby was sent to hell.'

'And the girl?' Grout asked.

Cardinal shrugged. 'She was probably tied in with Rigby. And knew too much for her own health. Just like Gilbert, Clifford would have traced her easily enough. And now she's dead. He's tied up the loose ends, it seems.'

'That still doesn't explain what Rigby was doing up there at Chesters.'

Cardinal nodded. 'That's why I'd like to go through all the shots that Gilbert took in that area. I don't know what we'll be looking for, but who knows what'll turn up? Maybe he'll have photographed something that'll give us a lead. We know he went into the storeroom; he might have shot something that'll help us with the cataloguing ... because I still have a gut feeling there was something in that storeroom that Rigby – and maybe Clifford too – wanted. We'll need to check his photographs against the list you tell me that young man Proud gave you.'

He led the way out of the house and stood in the driveway, sniffing at the air. 'First thing, we'll get a statement out of Gilbert. He'll be our guest for the night in the nick. By morning he might have cleared his mind a bit and come up with something else for us. Me, I'm off back to London. There's a conference with the Mets to attend. We'll be going over the cock-up that let Gus Clifford dance free. The whisper now is that he's probably already left the country. There are signs that his organization is being wound up: the rats are scattering.'

He turned back to Grout.

'While I'm down south you get on with the footslogging. Check the photographs, check at Chesters again … you know the drill. We don't want to miss anything relevant. We need to know exactly why Rigby was at Chesters. So concentrate on that. It will probably take time. The Roman Wall wasn't built in a day, you know.'

Grout was aware that Cardinal's classical allusions were few and far between, and usually inaccurate. There must have been something in his eyes that exposed his views to Cardinal.

The senior officer scowled contemptuously. 'Ah, hell. You know that stuff is all Greek to me!'

CHAPTER SEVEN

G ROUT SPENT MOST of the next morning working through Gilbert's statement, and checking the photographs that Gilbert had taken during his wanderings in Cumbria. In spite of himself, he was impressed by the quality of the man's work but in a sense that made his task somewhat more difficult; the artistic arrangements and the effects of light and shade often did little to help identification of the actual sites, and he was forced to check through Gilbert's notes carefully, to ensure he could match up the photographs with the noted locations.

By the end of the morning, he had set aside some forty prints which seemed to have come from the storeroom at Chesters and other areas in the close vicinity of the Roman fort. Armed with these, he set out once more for Chollerford. He stopped for lunch at Scotch Corner, then drove north up into the Cumbrian hills. It was a bright afternoon, with occasional clouds that darkened the fells with patches of shadow, and as he drove he caught occasional glimpses of buzzards circling on the upward spirals of warm air and sparrowhawks hovering at the roadside, searching for roadkill. He arrived at Chesters in the mid-afternoon.

The curator was helpful, even accommodating. It seemed he

had been energized by the killing at the fort; the death of Rigby had caused an increase in visitors, all wanting to get a glimpse of the site where a man had lost his life in suspicious circumstances. The curator was more than pleased to offer what further assistance he could … the result might mean an even greater surge in popularity for visitors to the site. The macabre nature of the renewed interest seemed to have escaped him.

'Who knows?' he said almost gleefully. 'You might even find another body.'

He was joking, of course, Grout concluded. One was enough to get on with. 'If you can just check these prints with me and note whether what we see in them is still in the storeroom, that could be of great help.'

The curator preceded him into the downstairs storeroom and together they checked the prints against the articles that remained in the storeroom. The curator identified some items as having been held in the main exhibition room upstairs; meticulously he then checked through the others as Grout ticked them off on the list he was compiling.

'You were here, I suppose, when Gilbert was doing this work?' Grout asked.

The curator wrinkled his brow. 'Some of the time. I had other things to attend to, you understand, but I came down from time to time to check on what Mr Gilbert was up to. He took quite a long time, as I recall. He just didn't take shots at random. He moved some stuff so he could get a better angle or whatever. He had lights set up down here, of course, and was much concerned with the shadows that he arranged. And in that corner …'

Grout looked at him. The curator's lips were pursed in thought. 'I remember he was particularly fussed about that far corner. The lintel was a problem, and though he wanted to take a photograph of the item there in the end he gave up. He moved the piece, finally, and set it up over there, as I recall, and …' His voice died away as uncertainty crept into his tone. 'Can I see that print again?'

'Which one?'

'The one of the Mithraic head.'

Grout frowned. 'It's not one of the clearest shots he took. This one, you mean?'

'Yes, that's the one. Except …'

'What?'

'Well, he took this close-up of the Mithraic head, but there was something else, here you can see it in the photograph, that he used as a sort of background, so it's not very clear.'

'It's called an artistic arrangement,' Grout observed cynically. 'The item is not supposed to be in focus.'

The curator frowned. 'Yes, but you see the focus is too … wrong, to be able to make out the lettering on that military piece. It's half-hidden by the head itself, and the lettering, all you can make out really is DI, and just there VE …'

'So what's important about that?' Grout asked sceptically.

'Well, I don't know. It's a legionary piece, of course, of little intrinsic importance, for finds like these have been common along the Wall, but there's something about it I should remember, something that struck me at the time, when we moved it for Mr Gilbert's use …'

'I don't follow you,' Grout muttered.

'No. That's right,' the curator murmured in a mystified tone. 'But as you see from this photograph it's quite a heavy piece. In some ways it's a typical item of statuary, some two feet high, the man thick-wristed, heavy-jowled, quite typical of the period. I remember thinking at the time, though, it should not really have been down here in the storeroom, it's in a decent condition, but I suppose it was down here because no one had got round to determining its provenance. At least, that's what I was thinking, but I was still puzzled. And now—'

'So where is it now?' Grout asked, glancing around the storeroom.

The curator scratched at his ear. 'Ah, well, that's it, isn't it? We moved it away from that lintel and over here for the photograph. And there's the Mithraic head that Mr Gilbert was using. But the other piece of statuary ...'

'Is no longer here.'

'Can't understand that, can't understand that at all. It was a heavy piece, you know. And who would want to take it? I mean, as I said, it's not an *important* piece, or it wouldn't have been down here, if you know what I mean. You see, the articles down here are of unproven worth, doubtful provenance ...' The curator suddenly brightened. 'Ah, but, well, yes ... that will be the solution. Doubt.'

Grout waited as the curator smiled in self-congratulation.

'You've lost me,' he said at last.

'Well, that's it, you see. The item was down here because it was of doubtful origin.'

Grout wasn't certain he understood, for a moment. Then it dawned on him. 'You mean the statuary might have been a *fake*.'

'No, I'm not saying exactly that. It was just that, probably, the piece had not been properly authenticated.' The curator shrugged. 'It's some years ago, and I can't quite recall ... It wasn't worthy of display in the showroom and ... wait a minute ... there was a discussion of the piece, it was published, now where was that...?'

He picked absent-mindedly at his lower lip with his fingers and made a little bubbling sound. Grout waited, staring fixedly at the photograph of the statuary. The legionary was half-hidden by the piece of inscribed pottery, and Gilbert had caught the sunlight lancing through the room and past the pottery. Dust hung in the air, minute spots of light; Gilbert had used the theme in the title he had written at the foot of the print, a suggested caption: *Dust of Centuries*.

The curator snapped his fingers. The sound echoed in the narrow room. He turned to Grout, a smile breaking out happily on his features, delight in solving a puzzle. 'Of course, of course, I recall it now. I read the piece some four years ago. It was discussed in a monograph, that was reprinted from a somewhat longer work. It was ... let me think ... but of course, it was Professor—'

'Godfrey,' Grout supplied and headed for the door.

'Professor Godfrey?'

The female secretary was perhaps forty years of age, slim, flat-bosomed and decidedly making no concessions to fashion behind her horn-rimmed glasses and determinedly plain blouse. She bore an air of overall efficiency that stamped her as a career woman – albeit against her secret wishes. She looked at Grout with cold eyes, as though inspecting a species of unimportant worm and the dissection of her glance was underlined by the stony edge to her tone.

'I'm afraid Professor Godfrey is unavailable,' she announced primly.

'Where can I contact him?' Grout asked.

The worm having been dissected was of little importance. The secretary turned back to the pile of papers on her desk. 'I'm afraid you can't.'

'Why not?'

The secretary grimaced, and leaned forward, her nose like a

predatory beak, ready to tear at her insistently annoying prey. In a supercilious tone she announced, 'The professor has gone south to collect some of his materials and make final arrangements for his trip to Europe.'

'Where precisely is he going?'

She clearly felt it was none of his business, but rather than suffer his presence longer than was necessary she heaved a theatrical sigh and in an icy tone said, 'Professor Godfrey is undertaking a short lecture tour of Austria, Germany and Holland. He speaks at The Hague next week. He has specifically informed me he desires no matters to be raised with him regarding work—'

'This isn't work.'

'—and he then intends taking a short holiday, after which he goes to the United States,' she said, ignoring his intervention and almost spitting out the words.

Grout caught an odd inflection in her tone, a wistfulness behind the ice, as though she regretted that Godfrey had not seen fit to ask her to be a travelling companion. Secretaries often adored their bosses; perhaps this one fell into that category, one of hopeless, suppressed desire. The fact he had not seen fit to take her with him may well be accounting for her bad temper now.

'Perhaps in the circumstances you can help me, nevertheless,' Grout suggested in an emollient tone.

'It's unlikely,' she suggested in an ungracious voice.

'I understand that Professor Godfrey is an acknowledged authority on antiques, is he not?'

The eyes behind the glasses glittered, at the thought that anyone should even ask such a ridiculous question of such an eminent man in his field.

'Of course he is,' she snapped. 'You must have seen him

on television, even if you have never read any of his works.' She clearly felt reading of academic texts was beyond the capabilities of the inferior man standing in front of her. 'The TV people are after him at the moment, want to offer him a contract to do a series on his own collection of artefacts – it's unique, quite valuable, you know, built up over the years – but it demonstrates what kind of a man he is when he keeps them waiting for a decision while he takes a lecture tour, and then a holiday.… Apart from which it's my understanding that Professor Godfrey has no interest in showing off his collection – he said it would almost be like committing adultery to allow the public to fawn over his favourite pieces.'

Her eyes had widened suddenly as the thought of adultery floated around at the back of her mind. Grout decided she was a very vulnerable woman, as far as Professor Godfrey was concerned. And he could hardly believe Godfrey would have made such a comment. His secretary probably read romantic novels in her spare time.

'Well, I suppose as an academic he needs the money from his lecture tour—'

'Professor Godfrey hardly concerns himself with such fees,' she snapped. 'He's quite well off, what with television, and his private collection. I sometimes think it must hardly be worth his while to continue at the university, but he is a man of principle and feels he has a duty …' She broke off suddenly, frowned, glared at Grout. Almost defensively, she added, 'He's been thinking of leaving the university, nevertheless. I'd go with him, of course, he would need me.'

But you're not with him now, Grout thought to himself. He murmured, 'I'd really called to ask him if I could take him up on his earlier offer and borrow the book he had offered to lend me.'

'Book?' She was unconvinced, suspicious.

'Yes. He offered it to me when we met here on my last visit. He'd written a monograph about Chesters Fort, and Hadrian's Wall and a chapter of it was reprinted in book form. He said I could borrow it.'

She hesitated. 'He has a very good library.' She sniffed. 'But if he let everybody borrow from him—'

'It was his suggestion.' Grout smiled. 'He did offer to lend it to me.'

'He's not here to offer it now.'

Grout had suddenly suffered enough humiliation. He folded his arms and glowered at her. 'Look, I came here to take up his offer. The offer was freely made. If you doubt it, ring him, I'm sure an efficient secretary like you would keep in touch. However, one way or the other I *intend* to borrow it. And I'm staying here until you go fetch a copy. So fetch one. *Now.*'

Her eyes had widened at his change of tone and she was intimidated. He could see in her eyes the thought that perhaps she had made a mistake: he wasn't a worm at all. He was just an ill-mannered pig.

Grout took the monograph back to York with him. He stopped for a cup of coffee at a small café in Wetherby and glanced briefly through the text while he sipped at the hot drink. It was not a large work, with perhaps 10,000 words on the subject of Chesters Fort itself, and about another 5,000 or so on the museum and the treasures it contained.

He soon found the section that he wanted to check through. It was not particularly informative but it contained all he wanted to know and it gave the reason for the relegation to the storeroom of the piece in which Grout was interested.

The Wall itself has suffered the depredations of farmers over the centuries and it was only in comparatively recent times that the museum was able to identify and recover quite important items that had been scattered throughout Cumbria and Durham, and, occasionally, Northumberland. Among the many treasures, however, there are certain items of curiosity value. One piece comprises a legionary carving inscribed with the legend DIBUS VETERIIBUS. It was donated to the museum by way of a collection gathered by the Tapper family. It is interesting to note that the piece was at one time used as a mere doorstep in the Tapper home; it was finally handed over to the museum in 1925.

There can be little doubt that the artefact is a manufactured one, in other words, it is not what it claims to be at first sight. The stone used is quite different from that normally used in statuary carved for use on the Wall. Also, I am confident that the piece dates from a period considerably later than its appearance and inscription would suggest. The cement used to repair a crack is of a different texture than that used in ancient times; sand and ox-blood did not possess such durability. So it must remain an interesting, if largely unimportant puzzle: why would anyone take the trouble to forge a piece of Hadrian Wall statuary when there was so much more freely available and of true historical interest in or near the fort at Chesters ...

Grout closed the book, sat back and thought for a while as he finished his coffee. His mind was still churning as he made his way back to his car. He agreed with Professor Godfrey – why would someone go to the bother of forging a piece of statuary? Godfrey had regarded the piece as an uninteresting curiosity, but Grout wondered, just how secure was Godfrey's opinion?

The opinion was perhaps brought into question by the fact it seemed someone had taken a considerable amount of trouble to remove the piece of statuary from the museum ... when Rigby was killed in the vicinity. Were the two facts really linked?

It could be that there was a connection, but for the moment, Grout was unable to see what it might be.

He returned to headquarters in a thoughtful mood. When he reached his office he sat down, took out Gilbert's folder and stared at the prints it contained. After perusing them carefully, he turned back to the monograph the icy secretary had reluctantly released to him. He read again Godfrey's account of the museum and its holdings. There was something wrong, he felt it in his bones, but he was unable to put a finger on what was bothering him. He turned to Philip Proud's notebook and read the list written at the back. The legionary piece was not mentioned. Maybe it hadn't been there when Proud made his notes – in which case it had been placed in the storeroom relatively recently. Or was it that Proud hadn't noticed the piece, or simply thought it unworthy of attention?

Grout's head was buzzing. He felt he was getting nowhere, and he began to doubt the wisdom of trying to follow a lead that probably took him nowhere. He flipped over to the front of Proud's book, to check through the scribbled notes he had made on his thesis. Most of it was gibberish to Grout, and of course it had nothing to do with legionary statuary. The account in Proud's thesis was postulated on events in Italy, not Northumberland. His thesis concerned mediaeval Italy, not the Roman Wall.

He felt depressed. As far as he could see there was nothing further to go on. He was wasting his time. He had hoped the day would give him something to present to Cardinal, he could visualize the glowering look he'd get from the chief inspector when he reported what was effectively failure.

The thought made him bad-tempered. When the telephone rang he grabbed at the receiver and snarled his number into it.

'My, my,' came a light and cheerful voice. 'Wrong side of the bed, Grout? Or was it the wrong bed?'

'Proud,' Grout said grumpily, recognizing the voice and the inanity of the man's humour.

'The very same. I've been trying to contact you.'

'And now you've done so. I suppose you want your notebook back.'

'Hell's flames, stuff the bloody thing into the dustbin if you like! No, there's something else I wanted to mention to you. Funny, really. It's something I've been puzzling about for a couple of days.'

'Tell me,' Grout said, hoping he wouldn't.

'The photograph,' Proud said. 'The one they published in the newspapers. You know, the location of the place where that man Rigby got knocked off.' There was a pause. 'Well, not just the location, but that mugshot of the deceased. The two together … it reminded me eventually, the link … you see, I think I recognize this guy Rigby. The dead man. I'd shoved it to the back of my mind, but hey, out it popped again! Like some of the old fellers who come into my shop. Won't be denied.'

'What are you talking about?' Grout asked wearily.

'I told you. I remember seeing him before.'

'Get to the point,' Grout said. 'I've had a frustrating day.'

'Frustration … it's the main underpinning of my business, I reckon. However … thing is, I remember now. That guy Rigby. I saw his mugshot in the paper, but I realize now I'd seen him before. Quite a while ago, now. When I was still at the university.'

'That long ago? And you remember him after all that time?'

There was doubt in Grout's tone, but he felt something warm growing in his chest. 'Tell me.'

'He came to the department. Took me out to lunch. Had a long chat with me. Told me he'd come to see me specially.'

'*Specially?*'

'Well, he came in, told me he was a publisher's rep. But oddly enough he didn't say exactly what publisher he worked for, said he was a commissioning agent or something like that and he really seemed to want to talk in detail about my *work*. At the same time I got the feeling he was a bit vague about everything, he gave out very little information about himself. He didn't ring true somehow …'

Grout took a deep breath. 'I think you'd better tell me all about it.'

CHAPTER EIGHT

PHILIP PROUD SAT in his easy chair, cocked one leg over the arm, raised his whiskey in a cheerful gesture and smiled.

'Sure you won't have one?'

'This is a duty call, not a social occasion,' Grout growled.

'Get on, you ought to take one with me. Who's to know, except you and me? Fact is I'm celebrating, I bought three hundred copies of *Cindy and the Whipmaster* just last week – three quid a time, probably back of the lorry stuff, I don't doubt – and then the news came through that the Metropolitan Police have seized copies as obscene. Result? I'm sold out at twenty quid a time. So have a drink! We deserve it.'

'You don't exactly deal with high art then,' Grout commented sourly.

'Never said I did. Commerce is the game! Give the market what it wants!' Proud sipped his whiskey, smoothed his straggling moustache with a satisfied finger, and gave Grout a dazzling smile. 'Life can be good,' he purred.

'Until you get raided.'

'Hey, the copies have gone! Nothing to be found here now! Cindy and her whipmaster have flown!'

Grout sighed. 'I'm not interested in the porn industry. I

came to talk to you about Rigby.'

'So you did, so you did.' Proud nodded, put down his glass on the coffee table beside him. 'Funny that, I should have rumbled him at the time, straightaway I mean, but I suppose I was flattered and then nothing came of it and I just sort of forgot what had happened.'

'Tell me exactly … what did happen?' Grout demanded impatiently.

'Well, it was like this … I got a phone call, he called himself Barnes, not Rigby, and he said he worked for a publishing firm. He explained he'd heard about my thesis and thought there might be a chance his company would be interested in publishing the completed work. I was flattered, of course.'

'So he came to the university to see you?'

Proud nodded enthusiastically. 'That's right. And I didn't sort of twig that the approach was a bit unusual. I mean, normally, you have to struggle to get yourself into print. And here was this guy talking about publishing a text on an obscure subject … but I guess I wasn't really thinking straight at the time.'

'And this man Barnes—'

'It was Rigby, all right. I know that now. Like I said he came to see me, we talked about the thesis, discussed its publication, and he wanted to take the thesis away with him for closer inspection. Give it to a reader, he said, an expert in the field. Of course I told him I couldn't do that since it was still at a draft stage, the material was raw, needed polishing before publication and I needed to check it through before it was submitted to the senate. After that …'

'He didn't suggest you ran a copy off for him, from your computer?'

Proud shrugged. 'He did, but I couldn't allow that. I mean,

there're guys out there who plagiarise your work....'

'Even an obscure thesis?'

Proud bridled a little. 'Hey, obscure or not, I'd slaved over that stuff! Though it all seems so long ago now, a different world experience like, if you know what I mean.... Anyway, though he seemed disappointed, he didn't make a song and dance about it. Instead, he said they'd like to consider it when it was finally ready but meanwhile it'd be useful if he could read through it, give it a sort of initial going-over. I could see no reason why not so I agreed, and I found him a chair in my rooms back at the university where he could settle down and read it, browse through it. In the end he didn't take as long as I thought he might. In fact he seemed to concentrate on one particular section, rather than plough through the lot. Took him about half an hour, that's all, and he made some notes, but I was glad to see the back of him really because I had a hot date and I wanted him out of there. And somehow I'd begun to think he wasn't all that serious about the idea of a publication.... Anyway, he pushed off at last, after saying he'd be in touch again once he'd had time to talk things through with his managing editor. And that was it. He never did come back, though; I can't say I was surprised. There was something odd about the whole thing, I thought at the time. Nothing I could put a finger on, of course, and in any case it didn't loom large in my mind the way life was going just then. So I brushed the experience aside, got on with my life.'

The girl, Grout surmised. 'How long after that did the thesis get lost?'

'Couple of weeks, I suppose.'

'You didn't link the two events in your mind? The visit from this man Barnes, or Rigby as he really was, and the destruction or disappearance of the thesis?'

Proud wrinkled his nose and scowled. 'No. Why should I? I mean, if he really wanted to publish the book he could have waited, it would be just a matter of weeks, and then I was pretty sure at the time how it all came about. I thought I knew who'd stolen the laptop and destroyed the thesis, and why ... but are you now saying there was a link? That it was Rigby who broke into my flat and did the damage?'

'It's a possibility.'

'But why should he do that?'

'Why did he want to read the thesis in the first instance?' Grout countered. 'For that matter, how did the thesis even come to the attention of a man like him in the first place?'

Proud was somewhat nettled for a moment, as though Grout was denigrating the value of the work he had been undertaking for his *magnum opus.* 'Hey, you know I did get a spot on television, you know. I was interviewed as one of Professor Godfrey's students and I did mention my work then. I remember, the TV crew had come on site and talked to me ... it wasn't tied in with the prof's show ... and I remember thinking Professor Godfrey was a bit cool about it all. He even suggested I shouldn't have discussed matters of academic importance like that on the box. Huh! Academic importance! It was all right for him to prance about on his own programme, but me getting airtime was another matter. He was clearly miffed that I'd got a bit of the limelight. Still, I shouldn't complain, should I? I mean, he came through for me later, after the thesis was destroyed. Supported me before the Senate ... got me my MA.'

Grout was silent for a little while, thinking. 'I suppose Rigby could have seen you on the box,' Grout murmured doubtfully. 'But when he was reading your unfinished thesis, you say he'd concentrated on just one section of the work, is that so?'

'That's the way it was.' Proud nodded and sipped his drink.

'And what was the section he concentrated on?'

There was as short silence as Philip Proud concentrated. Then his brow cleared. 'It's difficult to recall.... Wait a moment, yeah, that's right. It was not central to my research really. A sort of minor section, little more than a footnote overall, a byway, not important to the main thrust of the work. A bit of romantic stuff I'd put in for colour ... you know, stop the academics who'd be reading the thesis from yawning too much. That's right. The section on the Sforzas. That's it ... the conspiracy to assassinate the Duke of Milan during his visit to Padua.'

Proud got up, pleased with his recollection, poured himself another drink, caught Grout's glance and raised an eyebrow. 'Changed your mind?'

Grout shook his head. 'A conspiracy to assassinate the Duke of Milan. What was that all about? Why would it interest Rigby?'

Proud settled back in his chair. 'Who knows? But that's what he read. It was all a long time ago, and I've kept no notes. But I still have some of the story in my head.'

'Do your best to tell me,' Grout said ironically.

'I won't be able to vouch for the accuracy of the dates,' Proud warned him.

'Facts will do. I'm not interested in dates. Just tell me what you remember about that section in your thesis. And we'll see what might have interested a confirmed villain like Rigby.'

Proud nodded, wrinkled his brow. 'Yeah, well, I suppose most of it is still floating around inside my head, in spite of the porn I've been reading recently. And in a way it was all about porn, though of a different kind. The assassination, I mean. Power, wealth, the pursuit of these can be kind of porno-graphic, can't it? Right ... so let me think ... Lodovico Sforza, member of a powerful, rich and corrupt family in mediaeval

Italy. Like the Borgias, the Sforzas have left their mark on history. A bloody mark.'

He lapsed into thought, smiling slightly. Grout waited.

'Yeah, he was a powerful man, was our Lodovico. Powerful, virile, and maybe a bit mad. They had to be, to succeed in that bloody world. He was a patron of the arts, of course, like they all were, those mediaeval dukes in the city states, but corrupt too, and murderous. Lodovico himself, well, he became Regent of Milan while his nephew the duke was under age and then it seems the nephew died in rather mysterious circumstances, at which point Lodovico jumped into the vacant dukedom like a cuckoo into a stranger's nest. There was a lot of chatter, of course, rumours surged around the city. Was he involved in the death of his nephew? My guess is he was. Hey, this was mediaeval Italy!'

He sipped his drink, nodded enthusiastically. 'Anyway, there's the nephew dead, Lodovico is Duke of Milan but he needs support and he runs around trying to get the support of France, and then, when the French king decided he'd like to have control of Milan for himself, Lodovico turned to the Holy Roman Emperor, Maximilian, but by then he's got plenty of enemies and he is destined not to last long as Duke. He died in prison eventually, you know, after he was captured by the French, rotting away in the dark. *Sic transit gloria ...*'

Patiently, Grout reminded him, 'You were telling me about the plot to kill him in Padua.'

'Yeah, yeah, I was coming around to that. There were several attempts on the life of the duke, I mean it was a natural hazard, it sort of went with the job. But one of them, the plot I'm talking about, it occurred when he was visiting Padua to attend a wedding, and incidentally to drum up support for his dukedom. He was away from his power base; it must have seemed a good opportunity for his enemies to strike at him. Yeah, the conspiracy, the plotting in Padua.... As I recall, there were five in the band of would-be assassins. Oddly enough, I can even remember their names. Trick of the memory, hey? They were called Bocanegra, Cardenas, Perez, Boldini, de Rivera. Funny that, me remembering such details about a relatively unimportant bit of the thesis. But those were the guys.'

'They don't sound particularly Italian.'

'Hey, even the notorious Borgia family weren't Italian, they came from Xativa, in Spain. But like you say, these guys weren't all Italian. Three of them were Spanish exiles. Boldini himself, he wasn't even a gentleman, it seems, though he was more than handy with a knife.'

Proud paused, screwed up his eyes, stroked his moustache in a preening, self-satisfied gesture. 'Yeah, that was it ... Lodovico Sforza visited Padua in the December of that year ... what bloody year was it, I don't recall, damn it.... Anyway, it was the year when his daughter was married into the Scorzi family, so it's easily checked if you think it's important. He had intended staying for the wedding but then moving on, except bad weather delayed him, stopped him travelling on. It gave the conspirators a few more days to plan their project.'

'You mean the assassination.'

'That's it. Assassination.' His face lit up. 'Yeah, it's coming back, I remember now, it was the 15th December, a festive occasion, a grand get-together in the Hall of Princes. A meeting that was to be the prelude to a bloodbath.'

'The conspirators—'

'Don't rush me! I've got to go through this slowly. As I recall, it was the inquisitors employed by Sforza who squeezed out most of the details from the conspirator Perez, later. They paid a lot of attention to his genital area as I recall, before he told them what they wanted to know. They garrotted him shortly after, when they were convinced there was nothing more to be got out of him. As for the story he told them ... it seems Perez had bribed two sentries to manage an entry for himself and the other four murderers through the north gate. They gained access to the ducal wing; they concealed themselves in the antechamber to Sforza's private rooms.' He grinned suddenly. 'Ah, yes, and there was Carlotta. You know, I'm surprised Hollywood never got around to making this story into a swashbuckling film. Carlotta Fantini. A lady of Padua ... a lady of some repute, doubtful virtue, if you know what I mean ... yeah, it seems she put it about quite a bit....'

Grout waited as Proud seemed to lose himself in thought, probably erotic. Proud sighed.

'Yes, good in bed, by all accounts. It seems that Sforza had made an assignation with the lady in question for entirely understandable reasons. He was a widower at that point; he'd been happily married, you know, to a lady called Beatrice, though that didn't stop him having two regular mistresses while she was still alive. She was an understanding lady apparently; didn't kick up any fuss about his lustful wanderings. But anyway, here he was in Padua, away from home ... and suffering from longings of the flesh. Which he was intending to slake with an encounter with the delectable Carlotta. Anyway, the assignation was made ...'

Proud nodded to himself, almost approvingly.

'The Duke of Milan now, he was a man of precise habits. The meeting he had arranged with the Paduan courtesan was to be at 1.15 in the morning apparently – after he had dealt with affairs of state – and Carlotta turned up at 1.12 precisely. The guards had their instructions and allowed her to enter the anteroom. There she got a surprise, she was seized not by the lascivious duke but by the conspirators. She was threatened with a knife, while Sforza was still preparing himself in the bedroom for a night of frenzied activity. He was reputed to be a man of prodigious appetites, sexually ...'

Proud sipped at his drink, waved the glass theatrically.

'He had quite a reputation with the women. He was a dark-visaged man apparently, sometimes nicknamed *Il Moro*, the Moor. And a predator. His ducal arms gave him another name, the Eagle of Milan. Anyway, his loins must have been itching that evening, one imagines, and his temper fraying when she had not entered the room at 1.20, so he opened the doors to find out what had happened to her. You can imagine him bawling out, demanding where the hell she had got to, can't you?'

Grout raised an eyebrow but made no comment.

'Anyway, as the Eagle entered the anteroom he was faced by the five conspirators. You know, Sergeant, you have to admire Sforza, the Duke of Milan was a man of courage and determination as well as sexual prowess. Or maybe he was just enraged at having his little *tête-a-tête* disturbed. Anyway, in the next few minutes he got through that room with only a couple of wounds to his arm and hand. And he accounted for at least two of the dead. Maybe the five conspirators were incompetent; maybe Sforza's bulk intimidated them; maybe Carlotta herself impeded them in their attempt to stab the man they hated. However, with Carlotta screaming, yelling, kicking, squirming, Sforza bellowing curses, fighting like the madman he was – reputedly – he got through that throng and was quickly assisted by his personal guards who burst in upon the struggle.'

'The conspirators were captured?' Grout asked, interested in spite of himself by Proud's colourful account.

'Cut down. Perez was wounded and taken into custody.

He was later racked, tortured to confession. Two others were despatched, I believe, by the hand of the Duke of Milan himself. But I can't be quite sure about that. However, one man managed to make his escape in the confusion. He went by the name of Boldini. Seems he had the sense to retire early from the fray, get away from the botched bloodbath and make himself scarce.'

'What happened to him?' Grout asked.

Proud shrugged. 'That's where the questions start. The attempted assassination was naturally a scandal, and much talked about in Padua and throughout Italy, particularly when the confession of Perez was noised abroad. But as for Boldini ... well, nothing more seems to have been written about him. The Vatican eventually published some archival papers in 1962, but they received little attention at the time. I dug them up when I was doing my research but they told me little ... and really it was all a side issue to my work, so I didn't spend too much time on it. Sort of romantic, but not essential.

'But I do recall that among the papers was a report from a certain Robert Buckingham who at that time had attended the court in England. An Englishman who, it seems, had been in the pay of the Duke of Milan. The usual Janus-headed spy, informing on both sides, Milan and England. Nothing changes, hey? Never trust a spy. Anyway, according to Robert Buckingham's account, Boldini managed to get out of Italy, and eventually made his way to England. Buckingham's account was precise and confident, which would suggest he himself might have had a hand in the escape. Probably for some sort of backhander, one would imagine. Boldini and the other assassins, they would have had some kind of financial backing from the enemies of the Duke of Milan.'

Proud smiled, caressed his moustache.

'Interesting fellow, really, the Boldini guy. He was a

stonemason by trade, it seems. Not your usual kind of gentle-
manly murderer. But he was certainly a man who was able to
grab at his chances when they arose. He managed to get out
of Sforza's chambers unscathed, and escaped the mayhem
– where Carlotta herself got knifed, though it was only a superficial wound it seems – by diving through the window and
scuttling into the darkness across the tiled roofs of the city. But
he didn't go empty-handed. Assassin he might have been, but
he also had an eye to his financial self-preservation. The story
is that before he managed to dive through the window onto the
tiles below, he also managed to sweep up from Sforza's night
table several items of jewellery where Sforza, presumably to
impress or maybe pay the lady Carlotta, had displayed them.
Whatever, he got away, bodily and in possession of a haul.
By all accounts it included an item of particular significance
for the Duke of Milan. Something he treasured because of its
connection with his deceased wife.'

'I'm afraid that rings no bells for me,' Grout admitted after a
short silence.

'Your historical knowledge must be on a par with your
pornographic leanings,' Proud said in regret, shaking his head.
'Sadly deficient … your early education must have been misdi-
rected. But you never went to public school, I imagine. So, I
suppose you've never heard of, or seen, da Vinci's *Madonna of
the Seven Wells*?'

'You're right. On all counts. I haven't. So what?'

'An interesting painting. It was a favourite painting in Sforza's
possession. Not least because on the left breast of the Madonna
there appears to be a pinned jewel. I don't know whether it had
some religious significance – mediaeval art has never been my
bag. Anyway, the jewel was much valued, and was actually in
the possession of the duke. Though quite why it was so valued

by him – I mean, he was a very wealthy man – escapes me for the moment. Something to do with his wife, that's right … But the brooch was said to be worth the ransom of seven kings. To us, I suppose we'd say it was of incalculable value.'

Grout frowned. 'Your tenses are confusing. A brooch, that appears in a painting by da Vinci. And it was owned by Sforza.'

'Exactly. It was owned by the Eagle of Milan. And it was pinched by Boldini.'

'You say Boldini then disappeared.'

'Precisely. Some of the items he pinched from Sforza did turn up later, from time to time … I imagine Boldini was forced to sell them cheaply to pay the necessary bribes to get out of Italy and get lost.'

'And?'

Proud shrugged. 'You tell me. We know he fled that night with the treasures. We know from Buckingham's account that he came to England. Sforza's assassins followed him no doubt, once Buckingham reported to them. They wanted revenge – and, presumably, what was left of the stuff Boldini had purloined. But the trail went cold from there. A long silence, one might say.'

'So the duke's possessions were never recovered?'

Proud shook his head. 'No, no, I told you, some of them turned up later. As for the rest, well, the only item that was ever identified as important was the missing brooch. It was never recovered. On the other hand, while I was doing my research and being sidetracked by this murderous tale, I did come across a piece of information which seemed, shall we say, irrelevant in its context? It was noted among the Vatican papers, a sort of side note if you will, that a man called Bollands died at Alnwick, some fifteen years after the Paduan assassination attempt.'

'You see that as odd.'

'Correct.'

'Because Alnwick is a hell of a way from Italy? I don't follow—'

'Neither do I, really, not entirely.' Proud finished his drink. 'But it's interesting, isn't it? I took a look at parish records. This Bollands, mentioned by the Vatican, turns out to have suffered a violent end. *Murdered* in Alnwick. I told you that Boldini had been a stonemason by trade. The son of the murdered Bollands, Simon Bollands, was also a stonemason; he followed his father's trade and worked on the castle at Alnwick. But when he was buried in his turn there was some sort of fuss with the bishop. It ended with the removal of Simon's tombstone. It seemed the headstone carried some kind of offensive inscription.'

'Did you find out what the inscription said?'

'Can't remember exactly now but it was something like *To the ancient Gods of Rome* ... that sort of thing.'

Grout grimaced. 'I can understand the bishop wanting that removed from the churchyard. Even so, I fail to see what you're getting at.'

Proud shrugged cheerfully. 'Nothing specific, really. Just relating some interesting facts. You're the detective – up to you to try to string them together into something meaningful. But they were all in the section I did in the thesis ... the section Rigby was so interested in. And, well, I did my own bit of theorizing, too, I guess.'

'Tell me.'

'Well, look at it like this. Boldini stole some jewels from the Duke of Milan and somehow got out of Italy. Sforza used his intelligence services and discovered from his English informant Buckingham that Boldini had entered England.

Sforza sent men after him. Thereafter ... silence.'

Proud screwed up his eyes in thought, squinted at Grout.

'And the next thing we come across, years later, is a statement in documents once held by the Duke of Milan that
a man called Bollands has been murdered at Alnwick, in
Northumberland. These papers eventually found their way
into the Vatican library, where I finally came across them. This
raises a number of questions, as far as I can see.'

'Such as?'

Proud flicked up a finger. 'First of all, why should Sforza
record the death of an obscure stranger in Northumberland?
Answer: in all probability the man was not a stranger.'

'You're suggesting Bollands and Boldini are one and the
same,' Grout suggested.

'The theory is not all that wild,' Proud insisted. 'Look at the
facts and remember that Simon Bollands, buried in Alnwick,
was a stonemason. Isn't it reasonable to suppose he followed in
his father's trade? And Boldini had been a stonemason before
he started hiring himself out as an assassin.'

'Yes, but—'

'No buts about it, Sergeant. Facts is facts, if you'll excuse
my ungrammatical construction. But then there's the second
question in my mind.' He flicked up a second finger. 'What
happened to the stolen item that the Duke of Milan was so
incensed about? It seems to have disappeared, not heard of
again.'

'Not accounted for at all?'

Proud shook his head vigorously. 'Never. It's quite certain
Lodovico Sforza never recovered it. But it looks as though he
was hunting for it, as well as revenge, when Boldini was struck
down. So one has to wonder, what happened to the item the
duke so treasured?'

He grinned at Grout.

'Which brings me to the last question. It hadn't occurred to me that I should link the two questions until today—'

'The assassination attempt in Padua and on Rigby?'

'That's right. But after talking to you a sort of link popped up in my mind. You have to wonder why a man like Rigby would be interested in my thesis, and in particular the section on the attack on the Duke of Milan.'

'So theorize to me.'

'Hell, no,' Proud shook his head, waved his arm in the general direction of the bookshop downstairs. 'I've got enough on my dirty little mind not to want to get involved in real crimes. It's up to you, the copper, to root around in these old histories to see if they're relevant. But why did Rigby come to see me? What did he hope to gain from reading my thesis?'

Grout was silent for a little while, staring at the young bookseller. Then he rose to his feet.

'I can guess,' he said.

Grout returned to headquarters in a thoughtful mood. He was rather disappointed that Cardinal was not there and was even more disappointed to learn that he could not be contacted. Grout waited for an hour or more then wandered out into the city for a meal.

He ate alone in a small restaurant in the city centre. The menu was Italian, and his thoughts wandered over what Proud had told him. Later, he walked towards the Minster precincts and wandered through the close, stared down at the foundations of the great building where they had been strengthened to prevent an otherwise inevitable collapse. The building had lasted for hundreds of years and so had the Sforza papers, buried in the archives of the Vatican.

Grout did not feel he was an imaginative man, though Cardinal gave him credit for being so. There were occasions when he was fired with excitement by mundane things, sometimes a law case he was reading would enthuse him by virtue of the abstruse point of law raised. And he felt a vague excitement now, not so much at the thought of discovering who had killed Rigby, and why he had been murdered, as by the realization that the dead man would seem to have unlocked a secret that had lain hidden for 500 years. For Grout was quite certain of it; he could not yet prove it, but he was convinced that Rigby had been after the treasured item stolen from the Duke of Milan.

He would have liked to discuss it with Cardinal. He didn't have the chance. Cardinal woke him early next morning, the phone ringing insistently at Grout's bedside. Cardinal's tone was sharp, his instructions precise.

'Shift your arse down to London this afternoon. And bring your passport. That bloody man Clifford, we know now for certain he's skipped. He left the country last night.'

CHAPTER NINE

For the proletarian and the hungry there was boiled beef and horseradish sauce, venison or boar. For those with cultivated palates there was shish-kebab served on flaming swords, or schnitzel. There were mock chickens available – boneless pastry carcases filled with ersatz chicken meat side by side with splendidly layered chocolate cakes. There were vegan options. Lobsters were being served for the vegetarians, lifelike but constructed from soya beans. The air was fragrant with the scent of flowers and food; the restaurant bustled with custom and conversations fluttered half-heard through the echoing room.

'Interpol expense accounts must be lavish,' Cardinal remarked with a hint of displeasure in his tone, as they ended their meal.

The man called Enders laughed. 'If you think this is lavish, go to one of the restaurants used by our members of the European Parliament. I don't eat here every day, I should advise you, but this is an occasion when I must honour the visit of English colleagues. I think it is of importance that I show you the best. Even the sandwiches provided here, you should try them. They are concoctions of fire and spice and dynamite, caviar and *pfefferoni*.'

'I'll try them by way of celebration when we get our hands on Clifford,' Cardinal growled.

'Ah, but before we talk further – and take coffee – I must make an introduction,' Enders said, rising to his feet. 'Allow me to present to you Signorina Carmela Cacciatore.'

She was advancing towards their table. Cardinal stood, and for a moment was speechless. She was blonde, round-cheeked, full-bosomed with the smooth unlined skin that well-made women seemed to possess and her smile could be described only as radiant. She moved with an easy confidence that turned heads in the restaurant. She held out her hand, and Cardinal took it, stammered, feeling almost that he should lean forward and kiss her fingers. She was Italian, after all.

And she spoke perfect English.

'Detective Chief Inspector Cardinal. Herr Enders has told me about you.'

'And I, *signorina*, have heard all about you,' Cardinal replied. 'It is a real pleasure to meet you personally.' He had hesitated over using the words *in the flesh* but had thought they might be misconstrued. His wife would have been amused if not surprised by the gallantry he managed to inject into his tone.

He had indeed heard about the woman who worked for the Carabinieri Art Squad.

In spite of its name the squad was not in fact part of the Italian police, but was attached to the military. It was set up in 1969, and given wide powers of surveillance, including wire-tapping. It had been organized as a response to the serious nature of the depredations that had been made over the years to Italian culture, a response to the organized looting of Italian artefacts that had been going on for decades.

It was to the credit of the Italian government that they had taken the serious step of giving extensive powers to the group to which Carmela Cacciatore belonged; there had been an upsurge in looting and black market activity as a result of the post-war rise in prosperity in the west and after the UNESCO Conference in 1970, a computerized database had been set up in 1980. Within a few years, the Italian organization had established its credentials, spread its wings, set up sister organizations by way of art squads in Palestine, Hungary and Iran. Carmela herself was reputed to have been instrumental in exposing and delving deep into the murky background activities that involved auction houses, dealers, museums, private collectors in Europe, America and Asia. The hunt for those involved in the illicit antiquarian network was now an internationally organized system.

And Carmela Cacciatore was at the heart of it.

'I have heard much of your work in suppressing the *tombaroli*,' Cardinal said as Carmela took her seat beside him.

'Ha! The Etruscan tomb robbers…. They sell what they find in the ancient tombs to unscrupulous dealers who sell them on to respectable museums – many of whom do not demand details of provenance, merely in order to enrich their own collections,' she said with a wry smile. 'But it is an ongoing operation. And much wider than the poor families from which the *tombaroli* come. The families have been doing it for centuries. It is a way of life. We know them; we prosecute them. But the way to stop it and protect our heritage is to corner the dealers who fund the activities. It is what we have tried to do. But your own interests … they are not in the *tombaroli*.'

'That is true.' Cardinal hesitated. 'My main interest is in a man called Augustus Clifford. We believe he has entered the trade in looted antiques of late. After a considerable criminal career in other areas of activity.'

Carmela nodded thoughtfully, glancing at Herr Enders. 'The name has come to our attention of late by way of Interpol. He is a recent entry into our fields of interest. He operates from England, we understand.'

'The man has a long history of violence and crime,' Cardinal said grimly. 'We don't know quite when he decided to join in the rich market in looted antiquities but....'

'A rich market indeed,' Carmela murmured.

Enders nodded. 'DCI Cardinal informs me Clifford is suspected of murder as well as the theft of ancient artefacts.'

Cardinal nodded too. 'It looks that way. When he skipped the country recently, I feared we'd lose him in Europe – there are so many opportunities for a man of his kind to vanish under cover of a new identity. But with the co-operation and assistance of Interpol—'

'It's what we exist for,' Enders said quietly, 'and it is most useful that we can also enlist the Italian Art Squad in the matter of the tracing of antiques and those who traffic in them. It is why I invited Signorina Cacciatore to join us in our discussions. The Carabinieri Art Squad have been very successful of recent years, but as for Interpol, as you know, we have no police powers but as an information agency we can help in the tracking down of criminals, not least those involved in this international conspiracy of theft – antiques from Florence and Rome, Baghdad and Istanbul, lootings from Afghanistan and Iran – it is a wide-ranging business, as Carmela can assure you.'

He pushed back his chair, placed his hands on the table in front of him and leaned forward; he was a plump-featured, neatly-suited man with a hairless head. His eyes were like little black buttons, sharp, bright behind rimless glasses. 'I have put on alert my contacts in the German and Austrian police, and have been promised full co-operation. It would seem your man Clifford has been a little careless in his haste to leave your jurisdiction, he has used a false passport which was already on our files. With a degree of luck we may well be able to place our hands on him by tomorrow evening.'

'I confess to being a little surprised by your speed of reaction,' Cardinal admitted. 'I hardly thought you'd pick up his trail so quickly.'

Enders shrugged and gestured to the hovering waiter for coffee. The light from the ornate chandeliers in the ceiling glistened on his hairless skull. He remained silent while the waiter served them.

'Chance played its part,' he said at last, almost apologetically. 'As you know, the organizations that have linked together to form a ring, dealing with unprovenanced art works, have been successful for some years.'

'We know them as the *cordata*,' Carmela said. 'They stretch like a twisted rope, and their membership extends into many high places, as well as among the *tombaroli*.'

'And our endeavours have been frustrated in many ways. This was partly because Switzerland and Germany lacked specialists dealing with such matters, partly because we had no over-arching organization that could co-ordinate our individual systems; and not least because we were facing large, reputable museums who were reluctant to admit that they had been indulging in such trade nor to confess to holdings that were of suspect provenance.'

'The difficulties are great. The museums live in a competitive, secret world of their own, and there are many curators who seek only the glory of their collections, without worrying too much about where the artefacts may have been looted – to the despair and fury of the archaeological world.'

Enders nodded agreement, paused and sipped thoughtfully at his coffee. 'Still, there was considerable impetus gained
when the Italian government decided to set up their Art Squad
under the direction of Signorina Carmela Cacciatore … indeed,
I believe that the squad has recently been reinforced by a
compatriot of yours, a Mr Arnold Landon.'

'Our paths haven't crossed,' Cardinal admitted.

'He is an important acquisition,' Carmela added. 'He has
considerable experience. Of recent months we have managed
to assist Interpol with information in tracing some 500 valuable
antiques and paintings in Switzerland, Germany, Canada
and the United States. Two successful prosecutions have been
brought in Italy against individuals who played a leading role
in this international art conspiracy, we've built up a blacklist
of agents handling such works and we are currently co-oper-
ating in the investigation of individuals we believe have been
involved in the handling of items from the looted Baghdad
Museum and the thefts arising during the Libyan uprising.'

'I'd heard you'd made a number of arrests.'

'That is so. One in particular will be of interest to you. He
is an individual called Alberto Severini, on whom we found a
considerable number of incriminating documents which told
us he had been dealing extensively with agents in England.
He is not particularly interested in spending a long time in
prison, and a little persuasion, some direct threats, and the
prospect of a long period behind stone walls have led him to
co-operate. He admitted finally that much of his dealings have
been with a man called Augustus Clifford, in London. Mr
Landon, my colleague, is presently in the north of England, an
area with which he is familiar, extending our enquiries into
the provenance of particular artefacts. And he has reported
to us the name of Mr Augustus Clifford as someone probably

recently involved in looted antiquities at country houses in Northumberland.'

Gus Clifford. Cardinal felt his stomach knotting. It could be that he would soon be able to nail his old enemy for good.

Enders was adding cream to his coffee and he watched it swirl, thick and white on the black surface.

He continued, 'This is why we were able to put a trace on Clifford almost immediately he left England. In a sense he was already in our purview, as a result of Signorina Cacciatore's squad activity. We were expecting to advise Scotland Yard to bring him in within the next few weeks, and then when it came to our attention that there was an operation being directed under your control against him, we put some muscle into our side of things. It took us only three hours to learn that after he left London he surfaced in Berlin under an assumed name. We contacted the German police, a series of raids were carried out upon known receivers and that brought a welcome haul of items and information.'

'But you didn't get your hands on Clifford himself.'

'Sadly, no. He had already moved on.'

'But you know his destination?'

Enders nodded. 'We believe he is located near the Bodensee.' He sighed. 'This Augustus Clifford, he is an old adversary of yours, I believe. A slippery customer, as I think you would describe him in English. The Bodensee is a natural place for him. It puts him one step ahead of the forces of law. On the Bodensee, there are many passenger and freight boats coming in all the time, from Switzerland, Austria and Germany.'

'The traffic is international,' Carmela said. 'It is quite a problem.'

'Indeed,' Herr Enders replied. 'We have open borders, of course, unlike the situation in the old days and if Clifford is put on his guard by our early intervention and takes to flight, it will not be difficult for him to seek escape in various directions.'

'But you are fairly certain he has arrived here, on the Bodensee?' Cardinal asked.

'Do not be so anxious, my friend. He is not running at the moment. Something would seem to be holding him here.' Enders glanced at Carmela, smiled and sipped at his coffee. 'He is here, we are sure of it. He is accompanied by four others; they have rented a villa overlooking the lake. There is the possibility that preparations are currently being made for a swift disappearance but there is also the chance that some kind of *coup* is being planned.'

'Is that why the *polizei* haven't gone in on them yet?' Carmela said.

'Something like that. First, there is some kind of dispute over paperwork, you know how bureaucrats can delay things, warrants, search documents, that kind of thing. And if it involves extradition there are other desks papers must cross. Besides that, if Clifford and his colleagues are planning some kind of robbery, we would like all the fish to swim into the net at the same time. Precipitate action might cause the break-up of the group, and we'd have to start a trace all over again. The four at the villa have done little so far, and though we've inter- cepted their calls there is nothing we can yet act upon. Two left this morning and have not yet returned but there are no signs they have fled as such. It's business of some kind, we conclude. Observations continue, phones have been tapped, we have a trace of two mobiles, but we are reaching the conclusion that though nothing specific has yet occurred, it may be time soon that we move in....'

'Amen to that,' Cardinal said solemnly and finished his coffee.

Carmela rose. There was a thoughtful frown on her face. 'It has been a pleasure to meet you, Chief Inspector Cardinal. And I wish you well in your attempt to catch this evil man and put him where he belongs. But I have to make some further inquiries, which may be of some assistance to you. I must talk to my colleague, Mr Landon ... and there have been rumours in the marketplace recently....'

'About what?' Enders enquired.

Carmela shrugged expressively. 'The sale of something of great value. It is yet unclear what is involved. But I need to talk further to some of my colleagues; matters seem to be moving quickly. I will be in touch again, soon. For the moment, *arrivederci*.'

As she walked away, Herr Enders watched her going, clearly appreciative of the swing of her hips. He smiled, turned back to Cardinal. 'She is an able and determined woman. And a beautiful one. But do you know what her colleagues in the Carabinieri Art Squad call her? Though not to her face.'

'What?'

'Didi.'

'Why?' Cardinal said, puzzled.

'Because of her bra size,' Enders replied and guffawed.

Cardinal did not smile. He had the feeling it had been a sexist remark of which his colleague Sergeant Grout would not have approved.

Neither did he.

Nine miles away lay the south-west border of Germany; to the east lay Austria; under the hull of the boat lay the waters of the Bodensee, the lake forty-five miles long, 827 feet deep. Grout had read these details in a guide book at breakfast and now as he sat on the deck of the chartered launch with Cardinal and

Enders and raised his face to the morning sun, he felt again that he was a world away from his native Yorkshire.

He had never been a travelling man.

He knew the hills and dales of Yorkshire well enough but he had never desired to see the rest of the world; it was true he had taken a few packaged flights to European destinations but he still preferred the hills and fells of northern England. Now, as the boat surged slowly across the blue surface of the lake and sharp points of sunshine seemed to leap up from the bows, Grout could hear the conversation between Enders and Cardinal seated behind him at the stern. Enders was telling Cardinal about the commercial fishing on the lake, the steel-hulled fishing boats that set out each morning with their nets.

'It is a pity that you are not a fishing enthusiast,' Enders was saying, 'for there is good opportunity for sport here: perch, pike, trout, *blaufelchen*.'

'My interests tend to lie elsewhere,' Cardinal muttered.

Grout could not imagine where. He had never been able to discover what Cardinal did in his spare time. Perhaps there was no spare time. But he recognized the determination in Cardinal's tone, and perhaps Enders sensed it also; idle chatter was not what Cardinal wanted. He had his mind set on one thing only; he was committed to his search for the man he had been hunting for years and Grout guessed that Cardinal's palms would be itching now at the thought of being so close to laying his hands on Clifford at last. A conclusion to his obsession.

'You see that?'

Enders was gesturing towards the tall, three-storied honeycomb structure glistening whitely at the water's edge as they cruised past.

'Follow it along there, now, just there where you can make

out that terrace, and the road slicing up the hillside. Up above is the villa I've been talking about. There are housed Clifford and his associates.'

Cardinal was already lifting his binoculars. Grout had inspected them earlier, out of curiosity. They were heavy duty, Second World War, marked with the name of its German former owner. Grout wondered how Cardinal had come by them; they were heavy and inconvenient, and though Cardinal could have used more modern binoculars more easily, he was clearly attached to equipment with a history. He remained staring at the villa for a short while and then without a word handed the binoculars to Grout. After adjusting the focus slightly, Grout saw the villa spring into sharp relief; he could pick out the white-walled house clearly, and the low wall that ran around three sides of the infinity pool. Two men were lounging there in casual shirts and sunglasses.

'Neither of those is Clifford,' Cardinal said.

'You can tell from here?' Grout asked in surprise.

'I can tell.'

Enders leaned forward. 'I mentioned earlier that two of the party have left the villa. One of them could be Clifford, but I'm not sure. As soon as they return—'

'We must move in,' Cardinal interrupted sharply. 'I've waited long enough for this chance. As soon as the two return we must move in and take them all.'

'I think you are right,' Enders replied, even though his tone displayed some unease. 'We must hope that everything is ready and in place.'

In the event, the action was long delayed. The morning wore on, the sun climbed high in the sky and Enders made a pretence of fishing as the boat rocked gently on the lake surface, ruffled only slightly by the light breeze. The open deck was hot, and Grout slipped under cover of the wheelhouse from time to time, worried that the fairness of his skin could cause him suffering that evening if he stayed in the full glare of the sun too long. Enders trailed his desultory, un-baited line. Cardinal stared doggedly at the villa half a mile away, his attention riveted, looking for signs of movement.

In the late afternoon they received their first radio communication. Enders immediately snapped open his mobile phone and made a call. Grout could hear the faint voice of Enders's informant. He had no idea where the man was located but he clearly had a view of the access road to the villa.

'One man has returned.'

'He came alone?' Enders asked.

'One man only in a car.'

Cardinal gnawed at his lip. Enders glanced at him, waited.

'What do the local police want to do?' Cardinal asked.

'They are prepared to act on your instructions. It's unusual, but it seems you have good contacts and in spite of their misgivings, they will do as you decide. This will be an extradition matter, though we can use the European warrants. They have already told me that though they have the passport identifications, they do not know whether these men have forged their identities ... or indeed, have multiple passports. But, when you say we enter, they will do so. It's up to you.'

Grout was surprised to see indecision in Cardinal's eyes, he knew Cardinal desperately wanted Clifford to be in the villa before the raid occurred, but at the moment he could not be sure the big fish was there. So they waited.

The sun began to dip. Shadows grew longer around the lake and the surface of the water took on a deeper, darker blue. There were fewer boats standing out in the lake now and twinkling lights began to appear along the lakeside.

165

Cardinal's lips drew back over his teeth in a feral snarl. 'We can't wait any longer. There are three men in there. Once darkness falls the task becomes more difficult. We'll go in and take them. I just hope one of them will be Clifford.'

They need luck, Grout thought.

Enders immediately made the call as the launch on which they had been waiting nosed back towards the lakeside. They had a rendezvous point and the boat engine roared throatily into life and the bows lifted as the launch surged towards the shoreline. Cardinal's shoulders were hunched; he was uncertain, concerned, and Grout shared his concerns: the net wasn't tight enough.

They could not be sure their quarry awaited them in the villa.

From the terrace below the villa they could see the broad sweep of the lake, fading blackly into the distance but ringed with jewelled lights, coruscating in the darkness. Grout and Cardinal were walking behind the uniformed German police group; officially they could take no part in this action although it sprang from their presence, in effect.

The non-combatant role had an unsettling effect upon Grout and he suspected that Cardinal also found it irksome not to feel directly involved in the action. But there was little they could do; it was all up to the German police presence. Once the arrests had been carried out Cardinal and Grout could come into their own.

Grout watched while the men were deployed up the terrace towards the gate of the villa. Cardinal spoke from just in front of him.

'What do you think, Grout?'

'It looks efficient, sir.'

'Mmm. But unimaginative. What would you do if you were

in there with this little pack marching up on you?'

'I'd try the back exit, obviously.'

'I wouldn't,' Cardinal said curtly.

'The men in there wouldn't know the back is covered.'

'If they've got any sense they'd guess it was, though. I would. So I'd stay well away from the back wall. So what would they do?'

The detective sergeant was silent for a little while.

'The roof,' he said.

'Right.'

'It can't be covered, though,' Grout protested. 'We can't place anyone up there and I shouldn't think there's any way a man could get off that roof, even if he did climb up from inside.'

'No, I don't think it's possible either but we don't *know*, do we?'

Grout hesitated and glanced towards the policemen moving up the steps of the villa.

'You think I should make a check, sir?'

'I'm not carrying on this conversation for the sake of it, Grout. What are you still doing here?'

Grout left at once, smarting.

He was angry. Cardinal had that effect on him, the grating of two personalities who would never see eye to eye in human terms. But their brief experience in working together had brought its rewards in terms of success. It made it no easier to accept their basic incompatibility, nevertheless.

Grout's anger cooled as he walked down the hill and made his way through the narrow street, for he recognized also that Cardinal was right. It would be difficult to make the suggestion to the German police; this was their affair. And Cardinal would have to be there when they entered the villa. But the roof ought to be checked; Cardinal could be right.

Moments later he knew Cardinal was right.

Grout came back up the hill and found himself in a narrow alley that ran alongside the villa.

The roof was high above his head and anyone dropping from it would risk a broken leg or worse. On the other hand it was a flat roof; it would allow a man a running jump, and the roof of the dark building on Grout's right, though gabled, was only twelve feet distant at its high point. Grout walked the length of the alley, staring upwards. In a matter of minutes the police would be entering the villa. If there was to be any break out by the men within, it would occur very soon now. There was no time to go back, warn the police or Cardinal. He had to act himself.

A convenient pipe took him to the first gable on the roof; from there he was able to scramble across the tiles to a flat area where he commanded a view of the roof of the villa, slightly above him. He crouched down and waited, checking his watch as he did so.

His wait proved short in duration. He heard no whistles and no noise of forcible entry but not three minutes after he had crouched down, he saw a brief flash of light in the air, a window or a skylight opening to the villa roof. After a moment he thought he heard a confused thudding sound but could not be sure. There was the chance that it was the noise of a fracas inside the villa, with the police attempting to overpower the men they sought but such theorizing was thrust from Grout's mind the moment he caught sight of the dark, swiftly moving figure on the roof of the villa.

The man came quickly, light on his feet. He stepped to the edge of the villa roof and stared down into the alleyway. For a moment Grout thought that the fugitive was going to chance the drop; if he had done so Grout wouldn't have followed him for disaster would be inevitable. The man on the villa roof came to the same conclusion and with a swift glance behind him, began to cast along the roof like a hound seeking a scent. He quickly realized there was no way off the roof and Grout flattened himself against the gable as the man stared across towards him. Next moment the fugitive was stepping back, pacing out a run. Grout admired his coolness because it could be only a matter of minutes before the German police inside the villa came up to the roof in pursuit.

As Grout watched, the fugitive was launching himself into space.

He came down like a dark, ungainly bird, thudding hard against the nearest gable, sliding and crashing against tiles, scrambling and grabbing for hand-holds and for a moment Grout thought that he was going to fall back into the alleyway but the man recovered his balance, clung to the gable, and waited a moment to regain his breath.

Grout stood up.

The two men were thirty feet apart, and Grout was still hidden by the gable he had been crouching behind, but if he waited longer the man across from him might shin down a wastepipe to the alley and be lost to him. Grout stepped forward, his feet scraped against the tiles and he came out into the open.

There was no longer a dark figure against the next gable. Grout had not counted on such a swift reaction from the fugitive; he had hoped for the element of surprise. He heard scrambling feet, caught a brief glimpse of a fleeing man making his way across the flat area of the roof and Grout shouted.

He was rewarded with a bullet.

It came with a smack and a thud. It struck the tiles at his feet, across to his left and shattered several of them as Grout stood stock still in astonishment at being fired at. Not only was the man desperate enough to use a gun but he had even equipped himself with a silencer.

A black, unreasoning rage took Grout by the throat. He was not used to being shot at in the course of his duties. There was something altogether too professional about this turn of events and it enraged him. With a grunt he lumbered across the roof, heedless of the danger from the gunman, and gave chase.

He reached the next gable and caution had not entirely deserted him in spite of his anger. He kept away from the edge, made no attempt to expose himself and peered over. He caught sight of a vague, swift movement some forty feet away and ducked back to shelter but there was no bullet. He looked out again and the gunman had disappeared. Grout took a deep breath and surged over the edge, out into the open, dropping ten feet to a flat piece of roof and glaring around him angrily. The gunman had gone. Grout charged across to the gable top and looked wildly around him. Within seconds he guessed at the man's route; the roof of the next building was perhaps fifteen feet away; the darkness of another alleyway between lay below him. Almost without thinking Grout stepped back, took a run and leapt.

He struck his elbows painfully, barked his knuckles and the edge of the roof drove all the breath out of him but he clung, pulled himself up on to the roof and lay there for a moment, panting. As he did so he heard a curious sound, a mingled cracking noise and a muffled shout. He struggled up to his feet and in the dimness of a clouded moon he saw that he was again on a flat roof, extending away into the darkness, seemingly interminably. Halfway across the roof was a patch of newly laid tar, sealing for the flat area of the roof. To the right of it was a skylight. Grout came forward carefully and his pulse was racing as he waited for the bullet that could at any second come whirring out of the darkness. The skylight was broken. Grout knelt at its edge; it was perhaps fifteen feet square and the glass had been shattered. He glanced back to the tar and guessed what had happened. Whether the gunman had intended going into the skylight or not was unimportant; he had skidded while running across the new tar and he had gone through the skylight.

Grout licked his thick lips, considering his options. He could wait here, hope the others came along, or he could attract their attention. On the other hand the gunman could be hurt ... a fall through the glass could have cut him badly, and when he struck the floor below he might have further hurt himself. Grout peered through the skylight but could see nothing.

He put out his hand, felt an iron stanchion within the frame and then with his elbow he smashed away some of the glass. After only a moment's hesitation he sat on the edge of the skylight frame and lowered himself gingerly through the open skylight, bracing himself on the stanchion. Next moment he was dangling in mid-air, holding with both hands to the stanchion and the muscles in his shoulders cracked as he hung. He had no idea how far below him the floor might be. He had no idea what he might strike. He braced himself for the shock and closed his jaw tightly then dropped. To his amazement it was like falling onto a trampoline. He bounced three times, uncontrollably and farcically on his feet then fell forward on to his face. It took him several moments to realize that he was lying on an interior-sprung mattress.

He was unable to enjoy the sensation. There was a quick sliding sound from the darkness to his left and Grout rolled sideways, falling to the floor. This time his fall was more painful; the drop was all of ten feet and he realized he had been lying on a pile of mattresses.

A bedding factory; he was in a bedding factory and now it was to be a macabre game of hide and seek among piles of mattresses. There was the hum of machinery in the air but above it Grout could hear the clanging sound of metal, a gun hand banging against a metal door. Grout came charging out into the alleyway between two dark piles of mattresses, and he could see nothing but he heard the man at the far end of the factory floor move quickly at the sound of Grout's clattering feet. Grout began to run forward towards the doors at the far end where the fugitive was trying to get out yet once again, discretion made him step sideways into the cover of the piled mattresses. There was silence ahead of him.

Carefully Grout moved out, still seeking cover. It seemed as though the man ahead of him could not get out; if that was the case, he might turn like a cornered rat. Grout needed cover. Fifteen feet away from him he could make out the dim shape of a square, glass-walled container. Through the glass something glowed, whitely, swirling in an artificial dance. Grout moved quickly towards it and he made out three pot-bellied vats.

Next moment, the container starred crazily as a bullet smacked into it and feathers drifted out of the shattered opening. Washed and dried, like tiny ghosts in the dark air, but Grout had no time to admire them. He was on his knees, scuttling for the cover of the vats as he was suddenly aware that the flavour of the situation had changed considerably.

The man with the gun was no longer running. He was unable to get off the floor of the factory and he would have a little time in hand to make his escape before the police got around to this factory. Provided he could dispose of Grout.

So now he was coming after Grout. And he had a gun. The silencer spat again and Grout heard a violent clang as the bullet struck the vat. Grout lurched away from its cover and ran between the piled mattresses once more. He felt far from heroic and was now fully recognizing his own foolishness in coming down into the factory after the man with the gun.

He heard the steps coming after him, more slowly, more carefully and the realization that this man was a professional, doing his job with care, slowed Grout's own blood.

The man wasn't panicked even though the police would soon be here. It was necessary that Grout also should maintain a cool head. Iron steps loomed up ahead of him. He went up them quietly and carefully. At the top of the steps he found an unlocked door and eased himself through it. Beyond was a low ceilinged room opening up into another, piled high with burlap bags. Grout turned at once, realizing he had walked into a dead end.

He was too late. He heard steps on the rungs outside.

Grout looked quickly around. There was no weapon to hand, just bags, piles of soft bags, full of feathers. He could think of nothing less useful to repel a man with a gun. He looked up above him and caught sight of a chain dangling from the ceiling. He climbed up on one of the piles of bags and reached for the chain. It was looped into a hook, suspended from a trapdoor in the ceiling and Grout realized that the chain was used for lifting bags up through the trapdoor.

For a moment he thought of trying to force open the door, climb through to escape from the man coming up the stairs but there simply wasn't time. He could hear the man nearing the top of the iron staircase and in a matter of seconds he would be opening the door and there was nothing Grout could do about it.

In desperation, Grout unhooked the chain and linked the short hook at its end into the topmost bag of feathers. He clutched it to his chest and stood upright. The chain swung, creaking, the door opened and the man with the gun stood there, arm raised as Grout threw himself from the top of the bags.

The explosion seared across his eyes and he felt as though he had been struck in the chest with a sledgehammer. He was knocked off balance, swinging sideways on but even so he collided violently with the man standing in the doorway, and with a surprised grunt the man went down. The mouth of the bag was torn open by the fall and it spilled feathers in a cloud, a vast white mass of down. It filled the air, it covered Grout and the man underneath him so that they were forced to spit out the fine down as they fought for breath and for life. Grout was the heavier of the two but they found difficulty in getting to each other. The gunman tried desperately to free his right hand but it was the one thing Grout had seized for immediately and he now hung on the man's wrist twisting the gun away from his body, hammering the man's hand on the floor, trying to make him release the weapon.

A fist took Grout at the side of the head and the white down was suddenly shot with violent coloured stars. The two men rolled away from the bags and collided with the door. The gunman grunted as the edge of the door struck his skull but he gave no sign of weakening and he swung again at Grout's head, a wild swinging blow that lost direction and ended behind Grout's left ear. Grout felt the fingers of the man's right hand loosen their grip and with one final, grinding blow to the floor he succeeded in forcing the hand open.

The gun clattered to the ground. They rolled again, struggling furiously and the fugitive was underneath Grout but fingers reached for Grout's eyes, gouging furiously so that Grout was forced to jerk his head away. His reaction was enough to give his opponent control of the situation momentarily; he bucked violently and Grout lost his balance. He was thrown backwards against the wall, struck his head and once more crazy colours flashed before his eyes. In a daze he rolled, expecting a fist, a boot, some form of attack from the other man but there was none. He whirled on the floor, half-sitting and saw the other man through a haze of drifting white down, staggering away from Grout, but not towards the door.

He was crouching, bending, searching and Grout knew what he was looking for. The down impeded his vision, slowed him down but not long enough to allow Grout recovery of the situation. Grout struggled to his feet, desperately attempting to regain his balance in one wild charge but already he could see that he was too late. The man was gasping in triumph as he bent down, groping through the drifting down, picking something up from the floor.

The gun.

Grout stood riveted in the centre of the room, unable to move. It was as though it were a bad dream. It all had an element of suspended animation about it; movement seemed slow and agonized when it came, as though Grout were watching a slow-motion replay of a situation. The man came up from his crouching position and he was turning to face Grout. He rose to his full height, turning as he did so and the thunder of the gun was excruciatingly loud in the confined space ... the silencer had been damaged, or released when the gun clattered down.

The bullet went nowhere near Grout, it had been fired too quickly, in nervous reaction. But Grout knew that the next unhurried bullet would wing its way home, straight into his chest. He saw the man facing him, saw the arm raised to a classic firing position, the professional making the kill and the chain was to Grout's left. Almost instinctively he grabbed it, swung it and it described a dark arc through the still drifting down.

The second bullet went into the ceiling. There was a scream from the man, its thickening suddenly changing to a gurgling sound and then he was down on his knees, clutching his throat, making animal sounds. Grout staggered towards him, saw that the hook on the end of the chain had entered the man's throat, half-lifting him from his feet with its impetus, and had torn into his neck diagonally. From the spurting blood, Grout guessed it had torn the man's jugular vein.

There was nothing Grout could do about it. In a sick daze he fell to his knees and then lay on his back, as the last feathers came down, small fluffs of down. Just before he lost consciousness he was vaguely aware of the tiny snow-white fog that hung, lifted by a light current of air that was undetectable by him, so light that it could hold only the finest feathers.

Only the very finest feathers.

Eagle's feathers.

CHAPTER TEN

THE COLOURED CONCENTRIC circles stopped whirling and shimmering and a deep blue darkness descended.

Grout opened his eyes and the darkness turned to a dim, flash-lit greyness. He was aware of people and voices and someone saying, 'He is regaining consciousness.'

Grout struggled to sit up and found himself looking into the face of Detective Chief Inspector Cardinal. It was Cardinal's annoyed face, when his lean ascetic features seemed more drawn than ever and the thin line of his lips was marked with a downward turn that signified his displeasure.

'You're still alive then, Grout.'

Perhaps it was this he was displeased about. Grout put one hand to his forehead and groaned. He felt very sorry for himself and then he remembered the other man and the sickness came back to his stomach.

'Clifford?' he asked stupidly.

The displeasure in Cardinal's mouth became more apparent and was matched by his tone of voice. 'The man you were chasing wasn't Clifford. What the hell were you doing down here, anyway?'

Grout opened his mouth but it seemed pointless to try to

explain; he guessed that Cardinal's question had been largely rhetorical in any case.

'Is he … dead?'

'Very. You really opened up his throat with that hook.' Cardinal was staring at Grout with a vague curiosity. 'Self-defence, of course. I'll be interested to read your report on the whole matter.'

Grout struggled to his feet; Cardinal rose also, making no attempt to assist the detective sergeant. He seemed to be in a thoroughly unpleasant mood.

'I thought he might be Clifford trying to escape,' Grout muttered again.

'Well, it wasn't Clifford. The bastard wasn't at the villa. This man, the guy whose lights you put out, he was apparently called Schneider. So much we've got from the others we caught in the net, but that's all they're saying up to now.' He paused, observing Grout sourly. 'You were damned lucky we found you so quickly, Grout. We heard the rumpus the pair of you raised and came running, thought you might need assistance.' Cardinal pulled a face. 'You could have tried something less messy in your methods of self-defence. And more efficient, too. This chap Schneider will have nothing to tell us now.'

Grout swallowed hard, fighting off the nausea that still affected him and ignoring the throbbing of his skull. 'There might be something on him that'll be useful to us, sir.'

'There might be,' Cardinal said coldly, 'but you'll be glad to hear that the German police are looking though his pockets. I shouldn't think you'd want to be doing that. There's blood everywhere.'

Grout was sick in the corner of the room.

They returned to the villa within half an hour. There seemed to be a lot of noise upstairs, a group of investigators were combing the building. Schneider's pockets had been emptied but they discovered there was little there of assistance to them, except his pocket-book. The interrogation of the men arrested at the villa was being carried out by the German police and Enders joined them, leaving Cardinal and Grout to look through the contents of the pocket-book. It contained a wad of euros in a thick wallet. Schneider's passport was stuffed into the back of a separate pocket-book, together with a flight ticket to Schiphol airport. Grout stared at the photograph of the man he had killed and the photograph stared back, dark-haired, beetle-browed, neat collar and tie. It could have been the photograph of an aggressive businessman. Grout said so.

'Hardly that. A professional killer, it would seem,' Cardinal said, glancing at the photograph. 'And according to Enders, one of the best contract killers in Europe, or was.... So it's a feather in your cap, Sergeant Grout, if you don't mind the allusion. Mind you, Herr Enders tells me that Schneider's assignments seemed not to have been too numerous of recent months, so maybe he was losing his touch. You crossed his path when he was not on his best form. In decline, so to speak.'

Grout ignored the jibe. He was just thankful to be alive. 'You mean Enders *knows* he was a professional killer?'

'Of course.' Cardinal appeared surprised at Grout's inno-cence. 'But knowing the man was a gun for hire is another thing from actually catching him with one in his hand. That's why Schneider was so keen to put a bullet in you, so keen to get away. This would seem to be one occasion when he was carrying his gun and was cornered. Even so....'

He paused, glanced over his shoulder and Grout suddenly became aware someone else had entered the room. He turned and his eyes widened when he saw the woman advancing towards them. She was blonde, beautiful and more than well-proportioned. She was also clearly used to the impression she made upon men.

'This,' Cardinal said with a hint of amusement in his tone as he observed Grout's reaction, 'is Signorina Carmela Cacciatore, of the Carabinieri Art Squad.'

'Pleased to meet you,' Grout stammered, feeling his response was somehow inadequate, and Carmela smiled.

She turned to Cardinal. 'I have some colleagues going through the rooms upstairs. So far, they've turned up nothing by way of artefacts, or documents that might prove useful but it will take a while. We will continue the search. These people, they often have quite ingenious ways of hiding looted materials.' She smiled again at Grout. He felt overwhelmed. 'I understand you have had quite an adventure … and conducted yourself with bravery. You have our gratitude. As for the man who has died … he was not known to my people. But we tend to deal with fraudsters rather than killers. That is not to say some of our targets do not cross the line.… There have been suspicions about the villa.… You have something there?'

Cardinal was silent for a few moments, staring at the airline ticket in his hand. 'I'm just wondering,' he said thoughtfully, 'our contract killer might have had another reason for getting out so urgently. Maybe he wanted very badly to get to Amsterdam. Now I wonder why he would want to do that?'

'I can't imagine,' Grout said. 'Who are the others arrested in the villa, anyway?'

Cardinal continued to stare, almost absentmindedly, at the airline ticket. 'One of them is English, from Clifford's organization. I guess he's been acting as Gus Clifford's personal thug, and we've got enough on him to put him away for a while in England. I'm letting Enders deal with him, though, to see if he can pick him up on any offences over here. The other two chaps are Germans … I don't know where they fit into the picture at all.'

He broke off, glanced uncertainly at Carmela, then fixed his gaze on Grout. 'We've been concentrating on other matters. Grout … things have been pretty hectic these last thirty-six hours. We've not had much time to chat. I'd like to hear what you now make of it all.'

'All, sir?' Grout was somewhat disconcerted still by the presence of the beautiful and voluptuous Italian woman hovering in the background.

Cardinal waved a negligent hand. 'Yes, you know what I mean. Rigby at Chesters Fort. Eloise Parker at Sheffield. And now this little hideaway on the Bodensee.'

Grout hesitated, eyeing Cardinal carefully. 'You want all my theories, sir? I mean, adding what I learned from Philip Proud?'

Cardinal smiled thinly. 'Oh, yes, that as well. You've kept those cards close to your chest so far. So unburden yourself now, Grout, and tell me all. Give me the advantage of your intellectual curiosity.'

Grout's chin came up at the jibe but in a stubborn, determined tone he said, 'I think the whole thing should start with Philip Proud's evidence, sir.'

'I'm listening, Grout.'

'All right, sir. It all started when Philip Proud wrote a thesis in which he dealt with the assassination attempt in Padua, the attempt on the life of Lodovico Sforza, Duke of Milan. In that thesis he also mentioned that one of the conspirators escaped with a priceless artefact—'

'The Eagle of Milan,' Carmela Cacciatore intervened quietly.

There was a short silence. Both men turned to stare at the

woman from the Carabinieri Art Squad.

'You know about the Sforza business?' Grout asked in surprise.

'Who does not?' She shrugged, her dark eyes reflecting a surprise to match their own. 'The attempted assassination of the Duke of Milan is an historical event well known in Italy. How much of the published account is true, of course ... the flight of the Eagle of Milan, for instance...' She shrugged again.

Grout stared at her for several seconds, then slowly went on with his narrative. 'The conspirator reached England. Some of what I now say can't be proved at this stage but it's reasonably intelligent guesswork, sir. The conspirator was eventually murdered by Sforza's assassins but succeeded in hiding the artefact they sought from him. My guess is it was something he could not get rid of easily; an attempt to sell it would have been traced by Sforza's assassins, and would lead to him. So the conspirator kept it hidden. Bollands died; his son remained equally careful. The treasure of the Duke of Milan was never recovered. Then, after the son died, part of the son's headstone was removed at the insistence of the bishop and that's as much as we know....'

'And it was all a long time ago.'

'Yes, sir. But we do know that the stone was inscribed *DIBUS VETERIBUS*. That's the reason why the bishop ordered it out of Alnwick's churchyard. He considered it a pagan relic. And we do know that Chesters Fort was broken into and a legionary piece, also inscribed *DIBUS VETERIBUS*, was stolen.'

Cardinal smiled thinly, but some of the vagueness had gone from his eyes. 'So go on with your theorizing, Grout,' he said.

'My guess is that the stonemason Bollands forged that legionary piece, used it to hide what had been stolen from Sforza, and passed it on to his son. The carving, the wording, it was a clue to the location of the jewel. It's my belief, sir, that Joseph Rigby came by some knowledge of the artefact, or its likely whereabouts. He went to Philip Proud and conned him into letting him read the thesis. From that he got what he wanted. It was Rigby who broke into Chesters....'

'There's a hell of a lot of guesswork in what you say, but at least that particular fact,' Cardinal said quietly, 'is something we can prove now. Before we left England I read the forensic report from Newcastle. There's stone dust and so on among Rigby's clothing that links him with the break in and his prints have been found in the museum.'

Grout nodded. 'He was after the legionary piece ... which I suspect we will now never find. It would have been broken up to retrieve—'

'The Eagle of Milan,' Carmela murmured, with an edge of excitement in her voice.

Cardinal glanced at her. His tone was level. 'You have something to tell us, to fill in what we don't know. What is this ... Eagle of Milan?'

Carmela nodded. Her tone was sober, but her eyes were excited. 'The Duke of Milan, Lodovico Sforza, he was a notorious womanizer but it is said he adored his wife, Beatrice, and was devastated by her early death. She died of consumption, it is now conjectured. However ...' She paused, frowned slightly. 'You are perhaps not aware that Sforza was a patron of that most eminent man, the painter, sculptor, engineer, architect, scientist and genius, Leonardo da Vinci.'

'I knew that da Vinci had patrons among the wealthy in Italian city states,' Cardinal admitted slowly. 'But the patronage of Sforza—'

'Leonardo da Vinci was employed by the Duke of Milan as an engineer, to construct mediaeval engines of war. Eventually he came up with ideas for flight, and a submarine in addition ... but apart from that, da Vinci also organized Sforza's wedding to the beloved Beatrice, painted her portrait, and designed the wedding gift that the Duke gave to his new wife.' Carmela paused, and smiled almost to herself. 'A gift that, after her death, he took back and cherished as a memory of her. It never left him ... until the night of the assassination attempt in Padua. When it was stolen by the fleeing assassin. As the books and old records say, the Eagle had flown from his grasp. But no one seemed to know to where it had flown.'

'What was it, this Eagle?' Grout asked.

'It was an ornate brooch, including the ducal arms of the Duke – an eagle – and encrusted with precious stones.'

'Worth the ransom of seven kings,' Grout muttered.

'And now, of an incalculable value. An original artefact, designed by the inimitable Leonardo da Vinci and lost for five hundred years,' Carmela said. She seemed slightly breathless. 'And it would seem that the flight of the Eagle is now almost over; it has come again into the light of day.'

'You could be right.'

Cardinal grunted. 'Do we know what it looks like?'

Carmela nodded vigorously. 'The portrait da Vinci painted of Beatrice – the brooch appears on her breast.'

'The *Madonna of the Seven Wells* ...' Grout cleared his throat carefully, eyeing Cardinal. 'But I still have my doubts ... it could be that Clifford didn't know about the brooch. Not straightaway, at least.' He knew this was something Cardinal would not wish to hear. It would undermine Cardinal's conviction that his old enemy Clifford was behind all nefarious dealings in this matter. Hurriedly, he went on, 'Not at first. But I think Clifford did discover that Rigby, who was one of his hired men, was branching out on his own. Had some deal of his own going. He didn't like that.'

'He wouldn't,' Cardinal interrupted. 'I know the man. His gang would be under a strict code of conduct, and little ploys like lifting an item for your own purposes would be very much against that code. I'm still not convinced by what you're suggesting, but go on.'

Carmela again intervened. 'It is possible that Sergeant Grout is correct. There have been rumours for some time that something was coming onto the illegal market, something important, though it was not suggested it might be the brooch of Beatrice.'

'And Clifford would have heard the rumours, maybe. Got wind of Rigby's involvement in something big, and didn't like it. I think maybe that's why he called off the meeting he'd planned in London, either came north himself or sent someone, and when Rigby arrived at Chesters …'

'*Bang,*' Cardinal said. 'So you think Rigby might have got his hands on this artefact—'

'The Eagle of Milan,' Carmela corrected him quietly.

Cardinal nodded with a hint of impatience and addressed Grout. 'You think Gus Clifford then made off with the Eagle brooch?'

'That's my guess, yes, sir.'

Cardinal grimaced. 'All right, but just where does Eloise Parker fit into this scenario?'

Grout shrugged. 'It's not too clear, sir, but we know that she was in a relationship with Rigby. He must have told her to meet him at Chollerford so that they could take off together immediately after he had got his hands on the brooch. The plan was to disappear and live happily ever after. Gilbert, that photographer chap, he said she seemed to be waiting for someone. But when Rigby didn't turn up …'

185

'She thought about a dalliance with Gilbert, and then probably had second thoughts.... Actually,' Cardinal drawled, 'I can help you there, Grout, because forensics also tell me that she was out at Chesters early that morning. Before Paul Gilbert was up and about, wandering about in his priapic fury.'

'So do you think she actually met Rigby at Chesters?'

'No. The view of the local police, from forensic reports, prints by the body, well, they seem to think she might have gone up to the site shortly after he was killed. Maybe found him there, and then got out quickly, scared, returned to her home base.'

Grout pulled at his lower lip with a finger and thumb. He nodded, seeing the picture in his mind's eye. 'She came up, found Rigby's car first of all, maybe even found Rigby stretched out on his back with his head bashed in. That would have sobered her up well enough. And then she scarpered, fast. Wise girl.'

'But not wise enough,' Cardinal said. 'She shouldn't have stayed in Sheffield. Going to ground there might have been comfortable, familiar surroundings when she was scared, but it wasn't a clever thing to do.'

'I agree, sir. It all fits. She went back to the flat, frightened as hell, and laid low. But it wasn't difficult to find her. Paul Gilbert managed it, and so probably did Clifford. And it was Clifford who got to her first. He killed her because she could talk to the police, maybe even talk about the da Vinci brooch....'

Cardinal shook his head in doubt. 'I don't know. It's still too many suppositions for me. I agree that Rigby might have told her what he was up to in the first place. He probably gave her some hints, arranged for her to join him at Chesters before they lit out, got themselves out of the country beyond reach of Clifford....' Cardinal sat down and stretched out his legs. 'But that just about brings us up to the present ... and we don't know too much about why Clifford came out here to the Bodensee. Chasing after the brooch? Or does he already have it in his possession? Perhaps he's got the brooch and is meeting someone he could make a deal with. Maybe our friend Enders can help us out on that one.'

He was able to, a few hours later. The police were still involved with searching the villa but the men who had been arrested had already been hustled off to Constance. Enders looked tired; he had been mainly responsible for the interrogation.

'We have now identified the two men we captured at the villa. In fact, one is German, the other Swiss. They were remarkably consistent in their stories but Interpol soon gave me the back-up information I required to call their bluff. They are both dealers.'

Cardinal raised his eyebrows. 'Dealers ... and more?'

Enders smiled. 'As you say. They have legitimate businesses in their respective countries, but a great deal of undercover trading is done in addition. In items of doubtful provenance, shall we say.'

'You mean they're receivers?' Grout asked.

'I believe the traditional term in England is 'fence', and that is why they're here,' Enders said. 'According to them it was an arrangement that had been in place for some time.'

'Clifford was getting rid of some of his stuff to them?'

Enders nodded emphatically. 'These two gentlemen are among a group in contact with Clifford. They act as go-betweens with auction houses and museums. Clifford acquires the items, arranges for transport into Europe, usually to a warehouse in Basel and men like these then take over the items, cover trails by dealing amongst themselves, raise false transactions and documentation to provide plausible provenance and then sell the stuff on to respectable collectors or museums, through auction houses that are prepared to turn a blind eye to the shadiness of the transactions. Museum directors of the most eminent reputation can be surprisingly lax when they see an exciting piece that will enhance their own, legitimate, collections. I'd be surprised if these men are not already known to Signorina Cacciatore.'

'You have physical proof to back this up?' Cardinal asked.

'There is enough evidence in the house itself to justify our making an arrest and the German authorities are more than willing to co-operate in your investigations. They have already uncovered a considerable amount of property which would seem to have been stolen. As far as we can make out Clifford must have made regular trips across to the Bodensee, which was a useful location for the distribution thereafter throughout Europe and the United States....'

'And once the items were distributed, Clifford would fade from the scene,' Cardinal said grimly, 'with the artefacts under different ownership.'

'As you say. The pity of it all is that we have not got our hands on Clifford himself.'

Or the Duke of Milan's Eagle brooch, Grout thought to himself. He knew it was a thought that would already be burning at Cardinal. He did not voice it. Instead he said, 'Has any jewellery been found?'

Enders looked vaguely surprised and smoothed a hand over his bald head. 'Not so far. The material these people have been dealing with consists largely of bigger pieces looted from various locations in Iran, Europe and Asia, and international organization is involved. Clifford was the UK controller. But these two fellows ... the Swiss and the German ... they claim they do not handle jewellery. And I believe that Clifford would have fenced something like that in London, not here. The market there is a good one, I understand, though you will know more of this than I—'

'It's a good one, but I think things have got too hot for Clifford in England. He'll have wanted to do a deal in Europe,' Cardinal growled in assent. 'So these two men deal mainly in stone artefacts, antiques and paintings then?'

'That is so. Notably, of recent years, items looted from Etruscan tombs.' Enders stared at Grout. He was a perceptive man and he was aware of a certain tension in the detective sergeant. 'You have a reason for asking about jewellery?'

Before Grout could answer Cardinal spoke. 'Tell me, Herr Enders. Why was this man Schneider here?'

Enders shook his head and frowned. 'I do not know. He does not fit into the picture. The normal pattern. These men are dealers, criminals of course, but are not really known for what you would describe as strong-arm activity.'

'Unlike Clifford, of course. But he was at the front end of the business. Still, could Schneider have been brought along as a bodyguard?'

'We do not believe so. The dealers have had a long association with Clifford and other activists. They would not have had reason to fear violence.' There was little doubt in Enders's tone. 'However, Schneider's assignments are of a pattern. He is not a man who is hired to protect. He is a man contracted to kill.'

'But this could have been a rather different assignment from the ordinary,' Cardinal said casually. 'Let's assume that Clifford has in his possession a jewel of great value.'

Enders considered for a moment. 'A jewel of value?' he said slowly.

'Worth the ransom of seven kings,' Grout said in a quiet voice.

Enders glanced sharply at him and then at Cardinal. 'This is so?'

'Let's just suppose,' Cardinal said sweetly.

'In that case it is possible,' Enders considered, 'that Clifford would then find it advisable to have a man like Schneider.... But a gunman is still out of place here at the villa. These men, the Swiss, the German, Clifford ... they would have worked on a basis of trust, believe it or not, and Schneider would be a dangerous outsider.'

'But he was here,' Grout said.

Enders shrugged in puzzlement.

Cardinal shifted in his chair. 'Of course,' he said, 'Schneider may have been told to wait here for Clifford. Or to join him. Somewhere.' He stroked his chin thoughtfully and his thin lips seemed to reflect a certain inner happiness that surprised Grout. 'If Clifford got his hands on an item of such value, where would he go from here to get rid of it?'

Enders stared at Cardinal and weighed his answer carefully. 'I think we should consult Signorina Cacciatore on such a matter. Her contacts are extensive. A moment, if you please...' He took out his mobile phone and tapped out a number. He spoke in Italian; clearly, he was in contact with the woman from the Carabinieri Art Squad. He nodded vigorously, said goodbye and snapped shut the phone.

'Carmela Cacciatore informs me that she is already aware of the item you have in mind. She says if it is really up for sale on the underground market, for the transaction of the business, there is only one man Clifford could go to, and one place. She will meet you there, while I remain here on the Bodensee to co-ordinate matters.'

190

'Who is this man?' Cardinal asked.

'Signorina Cacciatore told me only that he is called *Le Cochon*... The Pig. And the location where she will meet you ... it will be in Amsterdam.'

The satisfaction showed in Cardinal's features. He smiled. 'So there we are. Schneider had in his pocket-book a ticket. A first class flight ... to Schiphol airport. So, Grout – it's Amsterdam!'

DCI Cardinal and Grout were met at Schiphol airport by Carmela Cacciatore. She had already arranged transport, and there was a barely suppressed excitement in her manner. They came into the city and drove in along Churchill-laan, crossed the Amstel canal and made their way along Ferdinand Bolstraat until they reached the Singelgracht. After they alighted from the car Carmela spoke briefly to the driver, who drew away from them and sought a parking space a short distance away. He stayed with the car while Carmela led the way to the man they sought.

'It is only a short walk from here,' she announced.

The three of them crossed the canal and walked along its edge. They passed some moored houseboats at the far bank; there was no movement on the houseboats and beyond them a number of cars lined the edge of the canal, perched precariously on the verge between the road and the water, seeming to hover among the trees that lined the road like crouching animals about to leap into the canal. Carmela led Cardinal and Grout away from the canal, and down a side street whose houses leaned in the upper storeys as though trying to catch glimpses of the traffic along the canal. Carmela stopped outside a narrow store window displaying a range of tourist trinkets.

'In here.'

She walked through the shop, brushed past a surprised assistant and opened the door at the far end of the room. It led to a narrow flight of stairs. There was obviously some kind of warning system in operation below because as they reached the top of the stairs the door opened and the man who stood there beamed a welcome notable for its nervous falsity.

'Signorina Cacciatore. Your visit is unexpected. And while I am aware that such visits always cause me trouble, you are nevertheless welcome. As always.'

Carmela glanced back to her two companions. Drily, she remarked, 'You will realize we are old acquaintances. Or should I say adversaries?'

The big man laughed nervously and gestured to them to enter the room at the head of the stairs. 'Adversaries, never, *signorina*! Too harsh a description! You know I always co-operate with you, and the colleagues of your group.'

Grout could understand why the man was known as *Le Cochon*. He was definitely of porcine proportions. He was over six feet tall and built like a massive boar. His eyes were almost buried in deep rolls of fat, his cheeks were covered by a bristly beard, sharply trimmed at the chin, and he seemed to roll as he walked. Even so, for such a big man he was surprisingly light on his feet and in spite of the edge of nervousness he had displayed on their arrival, Grout guessed that this was a man of a measured confidence in his business, and one who knew when to command – and when to co-operate. He clearly had considerable respect for Carmela, probably because he was aware of the investigative power she wielded in the murky world of illicit antiquities. And in his own sphere, among villains, Grout guessed he would be a man to be feared.

Le Cochon ushered them into the room. It was carefully

furnished, but Grout noted that the furniture was of a sturdy kind, necessary, he guessed to support the man's huge frame. Grout guessed the dealer in illicit antiques would weigh at least twenty stone. He had assumed a beaming, expansive smile, as Carmela introduced first Cardinal, then Grout to him. Neither man was fooled by his affability.

He waved them to seats, and as they settled into capacious armchairs, offered them hospitality. They refused the drinks. He did not seem offended. He smiled at Carmela.

'I must crack the whip over my usual informants,' he said, displaying expensively cared-for teeth. 'I had not heard, *signorina*, that you had arrived in Amsterdam. Normally I am kept well informed with regard to likely visitors to my domain, but this time ... I have no secret sources of information that tell me you – and your companions, English policemen no less – are about to visit me. Had you gentlemen not been introduced to me, I would have guessed you would be policemen, not merely because you are in the company of my old friend Signorina Cacciatore. For a man in my line of business it is simply that ... shall I say ... all policemen have an air, an aura about them. And the English police, they have the brightest aura of all. One needs to be aware of such vibrations, is it not so?'

Cardinal and Grout watched as *Le Cochon* waddled to a liquor cabinet in the surprisingly luxurious room and poured himself a liberal dose of Schnapps.

'It is a cliché I understand, that gentlemen such as yourselves do not drink on duty – and the *signorina* has never accepted a drink from me – but permit me to indulge myself. To calm the nerves, you understand. For Signorina Cacciatore never visits me for social reasons.... The room, you like it?'

He waved his hand to take in their surroundings. Its décor was as flamboyant as the man was huge but Grout had little time to enjoy it, for Carmela was impatient, and came immediately to the point.

'I thought I'd find you here rather than at your legitimate place of business.'

Le Cochon spread deprecating hands. 'You make a jest, of course, *signorina*. You know well that all my business is legitimate. I own this shop and it is necessary that I visit it from time to time in order to keep an eye on it. After all, managers are notoriously unscrupulous and one can so easily be robbed blind by people one foolishly trusts....'

'You come here,' Carmela contradicted firmly, 'to conduct under the counter deals, sell and buy items of doubtful provenance, and meet some of your less respectable friends. I know it, and you are aware, I know it. You see,' she added for the benefit of Cardinal and Grout, 'our friend does indeed have a legitimate business in the diamond trade here in Amsterdam but unfortunately he is of a weak disposition; he cannot resist meddling in activities of a more criminal nature. This is why we have become well-acquainted, over the years. I have not yet managed to pin him down to a prison term, but one of these days....'

Le Cochon gave a rumbling laugh that ended in a grunt of pleasure. 'Signorina Cacciatore will have her little joke, as always.' The big man was smiling but there was a wariness in his little eyes as he looked at the silent men facing him. He sipped at his Schnapps. His glance rested on Cardinal, calculating.

'I get the feeling it would have to be business of some importance, Carmela, before it will interest our friend here,' Cardinal murmured, holding the big man's glance.

'That is so,' Carmela replied solemnly.

'And you say that this gentleman conducts ... negotiations

on these premises. I wonder why he waits here today,' Cardinal said as though *Le Cochon* was not in earshot.

'It will be something big, I have no doubt,' Carmela surmised.

'So it is just as well we pay this call. For it might involve an artefact of great importance. A piece of jewellery, perhaps?' Cardinal suggested, pursing his lips thoughtfully.

Carmela sat silently, staring at the man with the glass of Schnapps. *Le Cochon* grimaced, spread his hands wide again, smiled, sipped at his Schnapps and looked at each of his visitors in turn. They sat in a tight half circle, silent for a little while. *Le Cochon* was smiling into his drink. At last, he murmured, 'A jewel, you say.'

'A very important one,' Cardinal said softly.

'Very valuable?'

'Worth the ransom of seven kings,' Grout said, as if on cue.

Le Cochon sighed, drank his Schnapps with a flourish and looked sadly at the three police officers. 'Ah … it is such a shame I cannot help you. Expensive, valuable items such as a jewel … what do they have to do with me?'

Carmela leaned forward, almost menacingly. 'I think we should not waste time in pointless discussion, my friend. We are here because it is my considered view that you – of all people – are the one most likely to be able to help us. But, if you feel you are unable to do this, perhaps I should remind you that there are certain investigations going on at the moment into activities in which, according to my colleagues, there is a suspicion you might be involved. There is the matter of a piece of pottery dating from ancient Greece; we are still tracing the route taken by the famous *calyx krater* and identifying the hands through which it might have passed. Your name has not yet come up as a member of the *cordata* but I have been considering adding your name to the list. Of course, that will mean we at the Carabinieri Art Squad will then be forced to undertake extensive enquiries into all aspects of your business here in Amsterdam. I need hardly point out to you that this will lead to police raids, disruption of business, closing down of activities, questioning – out of which may emerge much information important to us and damaging to your enterprises. If not to your health, you could lose considerable weight, in prison.' Carmela paused. 'Of course, all this could be avoided. We have reached an understanding in the past. A little information here, a little there … but if, on this occasion you feel unable to assist me, well, perhaps our little arrangement will necessarily have to come to an end. Trouble could well loom for you then, as you will appreciate.'

Le Cochon sat very still, staring at Carmela almost as though he felt a friendship had been betrayed. Carefully he put down his empty glass, folded his hands across his expansive stomach. He chewed at his blubbery lips, thoughtfully. 'You are very serious about this. '

'Very.'

'You speak of a piece of jewellery,' *Le Cochon* murmured. 'Of great value.' He held her glance. He sighed. 'It has not come to me, *signorina.*'

There was a certain hesitancy in his tone. Carmela seized on the unspoken words. 'You do not have it, but you expect it will be coming to you?'

Le Cochon stared at her almost in dismay. 'No, no, you must know that is not the way things are … arranged. I do not have what you seek… I don't think it will even be coming to me.' He hesitated for a moment. 'But … this piece … it is important … this jewel…?'

'We think it might be the Eagle of Milan.'

Cardinal glanced quickly at Carmela then at Grout; both men were of one mind. They doubted the wisdom of telling the dealer what they were looking for. But the piggy eyes of *Le Cochon* had widened in surprise.

'The *Eagle*? After all these centuries? I cannot believe … The rumours have been in the air, but it was never said it might be the piece you mention!' Suddenly there was an edge almost of panic in his tone. 'Such a piece … the da Vinci brooch. That would be beyond my range, *signorina* – you must know that.'

'But there *has* been talk in the marketplace,' Carmela insisted firmly.

Le Cochon was suddenly sweating. He took a large handkerchief from the pocket of his voluminous jacket and wiped his hands. He stared moodily at his empty glass and sighed again. 'Such an item…. Well, yes, there have been whispers of something big, something important. I have to admit there has been talk, and the dealers have started to gather.'

'At the Bodensee?'

'That is possible,' the big man replied, almost distracted. 'But I have heard only that there is an Englishman involved….'

'His name?' Cardinal asked harshly, unable to contain himself longer.

Le Cochon stared at him, vaguely, almost as though he had barely heard him. 'The Englishman? I am told, I have heard it is the man who….' He took a deep, ragged breath. 'I think you are looking for a man by the name of Augustus Clifford.'

Cardinal gave a fierce nod and leaned forward. 'He has the Eagle of Milan? He has been trying to sell it? Has he been *here*?'

'No.' *Le Cochon* shook his head in denial. He turned to Carmela, almost pleadingly. 'You must understand, *signorina*. The world I inhabit, the one you prowl the edges of, it relies on whispers and trust and *mistrust*. I had not heard it was a matter of the Eagle of Milan ... but I had heard the Englishman Clifford was in the marketplace with something valuable. But that is all I know, and I have not met this man Clifford. I tell you this so that you will have confidence in me, *signorina*, so our arrangements may continue in spite of the slighting remarks you have made of me today. I am an honest man. I desire only to assist the Carabinieri Art Squad, as a legitimate man of business. No, I have not met him, but I have heard that there is ... an artefact. One of great value. I have been asked if I was interested in bringing together some dealers, merely as a middleman if you understand what I mean....'

'I don't believe you,' Carmela replied angrily.

'I swear—'

'Don't perjure yourself,' Carmela said coldly and rose to her feet. 'You will be hearing from me and my colleagues.'

'No, please, we must maintain our relationship....'

Carmela stood glaring at him, implacable, and the big man wiped his hands again, and sighed. He shrugged. 'Ah, well, all right. It is of little consequence in any case. Yes, Clifford, or an associate of his, telephoned me a few days ago.'

'And you arranged to meet him.'

The little eyes flickered from the face of Carmela to Cardinal. 'An arrangement was made to meet. There were to be ... ah ... discussions. But he did not say it was to be about the treasure of the Duke of Milan....'

'You say there were to be discussions. They haven't taken place?' Cardinal queried.

'You must understand. It was a negotiation only. I would consider handling the ... onward transmission of the item, though I assure you I would have done it, only I was made certain that there was nothing illegal about the matter—'

'Come, come,' Carmela reproved him. 'You knew of this

man Clifford, and his dealings. It would have had to be a doubtful transaction.'

Le Cochon shrugged uneasily. 'A man has to live, *signorina*. But I am being frank with you. We were to meet. If all was well, there would be a further meeting.... Negotiations first, transactions thereafter.'

Cardinal frowned. Something was niggling at him. 'A moment ago you said that all this is of no consequence in any case. What did you mean by that?'

Le Cochon made no immediate reply but folded his hands once more over his huge stomach and closed his eyes. In a sharp, exasperated tone Cardinal said, 'Two people have died already and this jewel has been the prize. This is not simply a case of stolen goods, of receiving stolen property. This is a case of *murder.*'

'Murder? ' It came out as a grunt. *Le Cochon* opened his eyes and they were bright and red, gleaming. He made a negative gesture with his hand, rose with difficulty and lumbered across the room with a slow gait. He stared out to the street and the canal beyond with his back to Carmela and the two men.

'Murder, you say. This does not surprise me. The Eagle of the Duke ... so many years it has flown....' His voice took on a more thoughtful tone. 'You know, *signorina*, parking space in Amsterdam is so restricted. During the day, and again in the late evening, it is so difficult to find parking spaces. The cars line the canals and from time to time a careless driver does not properly put on his handbrake or engage gear. And it is not unknown for a car to trundle forward, perhaps slip into the canal. I have seen the result. Here, even, from my window. Do you know that Amsterdam has a special service, for recovery of such vehicles?' He paused, spread his fat hands wide. 'In fact, a car was pulled out of the Amstel this morning, at dawn, I understand.... There was the body of a man discovered in the interior of the vehicle. A report of the incident appeared in the newspaper this afternoon. It was accurate as far as my own informants have been able to assure me.'

'Has the man been identified?' Cardinal asked, as a cold feeling seemed to touch his spine.

Le Cochon waddled somewhat unsteadily across to the cabinet to pour himself another drink. 'I am told his papers were in order, and recovered. An American tourist, it seems.'

'What has this to do with your projected meeting with Clifford?' Carmela demanded, irritated by the big man's attitude and the manner in which he seemed to be skirting around the fringes of their questions.

Le Cochon shrugged, still staring down towards the canal. 'This *accident*, it tells me that Mr Clifford will not be coming to talk to me.'

Cardinal caught the emphasis on the word *accident*. He rose to his feet angrily and walked across the room. He stood, angrily staring out at the street and the canal. In a harsh voice he said, 'I don't understand. What has an American tourist got to do with Clifford?'

Le Cochon turned. His fleshy face was expressionless. 'According to a statement issued by the police, and the reports in the afternoon newspapers, the dead man's passport identified him as one Rudolf Kling. But my associates tell me that Rudolf Kling was not his real name, it was merely an assumed identity. A false passport is easily acquired.' He smiled blandly, savouring the moment. 'This Rudolf Kling ... you will know the man under a different name....' His little eyes were fixed on Cardinal. 'Mr Augustus Clifford.'

CHAPTER ELEVEN

THE AMSTERDAM POLICE did all they could to help but the information they could offer was little enough. Of the fact that it was a case of murder they had no doubt. The car had been discovered at dawn by a boat proceeding along the Amstel and within minutes, the police and the fire engines had arrived. It had taken them well over an hour to winch the car out of the canal and there had been nothing they could do for the man inside.

'How did he die?' Cardinal asked brusquely.

'Of drowning. But he had first been struck on the head. He must have been unconscious when the car entered the water. Trapped inside, he would soon have drowned.'

'How do you reconstruct the crime?'

The burly Amsterdam detective pursed his lips. 'We think he had probably met his assailant some distance from the canal, there must have been some sort of argument and as the victim turned away, he was struck from behind, at the back of the head. It could have happened at the edge of the canal but we cannot be certain. He was then dragged or carried the short distance to the car, placed in the passenger seat. The car was driven along the Amstel to a quiet area, the driver parked it at the edge of the road, pushed the unconscious man across the seat, closed the door and pushed the car into the canal. It would have sunk within minutes.'

'Is there no chance of finding a witness to what happened?' Cardinal asked.

'The area where the car entered the water is unfrequented at night. During the day it is used by lorries delivering goods to the nearby warehouses ... it is a piece of wasteland. No witnesses.'

'Whose was the car?'

'It was a hired car,' the Amsterdam man replied. 'It was hired in the name of this man Kling.'

'Clifford.'

'As you say. His American passport states the name Rudolf Kling.'

'It's Clifford all right.' Grout had been with Cardinal when the corpse had been identified by him and he had seen the blank loss in Cardinal's eyes. In a sense Cardinal was feeling defeat; he had wanted to get Clifford, it was an obsession that had driven him for years, and it had almost come to a climax this week.

Now, it was anti-climax and Clifford was dead. A decade-long manhunt was over. And Cardinal was left with a feeling of emptiness.

'Did you find anything in the car?' Grout asked suddenly. The Amsterdam man raised an interrogative eyebrow.

'Anything of *value*,' Grout added.

The detective shrugged. 'Nothing. The car was clean, it had been hired only hours earlier, so it had been seldom used.'

Cardinal cast a contemptuous glance in Grout's direction as though chiding him for even thinking the man who murdered Clifford would have left the Sforza brooch in the car.

'I presume your officers have already checked on his hotel, and searched his room.'

'They have.' The Amsterdam detective smiled. 'It had been hardly used. A few personal effects, that is all. But you are quite welcome to take a look also. We are only too happy to co-operate. Nevertheless, I am sure you will find nothing has been overlooked.'

The hotel Clifford had used was an expensive one in the centre of Amsterdam, much frequented by American tourists. Cardinal and Grout made their way through a plush lounge to the reception desk, introduced themselves and asked to be taken to the room used by Kling. The receptionist appeared embarrassed and explained that she should first contact the manager. She vanished in a flurry and Cardinal and Grout waited, eyeing some of the camera-laden Americans who wandered into the lounge. While they waited they heard a burst of applause from beyond large doors at the far end of the room and Cardinal grimaced.

'A meeting or a lecture of some kind. I suppose it'll be in Dutch, so that leaves me out. I presume you do speak Dutch, among your other accomplishments'

Grout made no reply and the receptionist returned with a harassed expression, called them forward to the lift and hurried ahead of them. She was a nervous, stringy woman, immaculately dressed but flustered. She was clearly not used to dealing with the police. She pressed the button in the lift and remained silent, head down as they ascended. When the doors opened a man stood waiting for them. He introduced himself as the manager, a small, edgy fellow in a dark grey suit and white shirt; his eyes seemed never to stay still, flicking glances about him as though seeking dusty evidence of cleaning staff incompetence. He gestured towards the end of the corridor, and led the way to the room taken in the name of Rudolf Kling.

He hovered in the doorway until Cardinal brusquely told him they would rather look around alone.

The two men worked through the rooms of the suite quickly and efficiently. Within the hour they faced each other and confessed defeat. There was nothing of value in the rooms. Cardinal sat down on the bed with a disgruntled expression, then lay back and closed his eyes.

'I don't understand it, Grout.'

Carefully, Grout slid into a chair and stared at his chief. He made no reply and after a moment Cardinal opened his eyes and stared at the ceiling.

'And yet, though I don't understand it, there's something in all this that we should have seen but have just missed. For the life of me I can't think what. But come on, Grout, you're the one with flair, according to your uncle, the chief constable. You're with me to do the thinking … I'm the honest plodder, you're the bright, self-educated man. So what do you make of it all?' He rolled over suddenly onto his stomach and glared at Grout. 'You theorized about what happened at Chesters and thereafter and I went along with that, but somewhere we've gone wrong. We've skidded off track. But where?'

Grout considered, thinking over the events of the last twenty-four hours. At last, hesitantly, he said, 'Time factor, sir.'

Cardinal glared at him, his thin mouth drooping and then he nodded, abruptly. 'Yes, I suppose it's been bothering me too. Not so much the time factor, as the timing of events. Clifford skipped from England and came to the Bodensee and then sat there. Waiting. But what was he waiting for?'

'The fences, sir?'

'But why couldn't he arrange for them to be waiting for him? And then again, he left the Bodensee yesterday, or even earlier, and he came to Amsterdam. Then he waited again, here in this hotel. What the hell for? He contacted *Le Cochon* but that fat bastard insists they were to meet only to negotiate. But what? What was Clifford up to? Was he hoping to find a buyer for the Sforza brooch through *Le Cochon*? Or did he have something else on his mind? And really, what the hell was he doing here in Amsterdam? What *was* he waiting for?'

'I don't know, sir.'

Cardinal growled deep in his chest as though infuriated that Grout could provide no answers. 'There are two other things that bother me. The first is that damned man Schneider. I can't understand why Clifford hired him ... though it would have been more than useful to have him here last night, hey? Clifford wouldn't have snuffed it then, would he?"

'Maybe that was the idea, sir. Protection.'

Cardinal snorted indignantly. 'You heard what Enders said. Schneider was a contract killer, not a bloody guard.'

'All right, sir,' Grout replied levelly. 'Protection and assassination.'

Cardinal struggled off the bed and began to pace around the confines of the room, with his hands thrust deep into his pockets. He looked decidedly unhappy. 'You know, Grout, it seems to me we're beginning to spin around in circles. I've got the feeling we've got bogged down in irrelevant stuff and I'd like to know where. I'm getting a strong suspicion in my mind....'

'I think it has echoes in mine, sir.'

The two men stared at each other. Slowly, Cardinal said, nodding, 'You know, I'm beginning to wonder that our assumption that Clifford was trying to *sell* the Eagle of Milan might be off the mark.'

'I'm beginning to wonder the same thing, sir. If he had

it, he could probably have done the deal he was seeking at the Bodensee. But he skipped from there, to arrive here in Amsterdam. And as for *Le Cochon* … maybe Clifford wasn't trying to arrange a sale. Maybe he was just….'

Cardinal nodded slowly. 'Seeking information. It could be that's why he was waiting at the Bodensee, and then came here when he realized he was wasting his time there. Information …'

'Or a meeting with the man who was in possession of the Eagle.'

Cardinal nodded thoughtfully. He remained silent for a little while. 'There's another thing. Let's go back to Rigby…. We've been assuming all along that Clifford killed Rigby. It would certainly have been Clifford's *style* to kill him for breaking ranks, but have we been too limited in our assumptions? Clifford could have killed Rigby, or got one of his hard men to do it for him. But who else might have been in the frame? If it was someone else, someone who killed Rigby, grabbed the artefact and got out of England….'

'Once Clifford got wind of what was going on, he'd soon be hot on his tail, along with Schneider to act as his persuader. I've got the feeling, sir, we need to start all over again, and question each of our basic assumptions.' Grout added.

Cardinal smiled. 'It makes a pleasant change to have us both thinking along the same lines, Grout.'

'Even if we're no nearer to a conclusion than when we started, sir?'

Cardinal's smile was replaced by a scowl. He continued to prowl around the room restlessly. 'You know what we'll have to do, Grout. We'll have to go right back, start right at the very beginning and take logical steps. Work through in progression … it's the plodding that brings results, Grout, not the flashes of intuition. We've got to work at this, look at our theories, discover—'

'The *non sequitur* ...'

'The what?'

Grout smiled at Cardinal's suspicious exclamation. 'Discover where we've taken a wrong step in our process of logical thought. Like you, sir, I'm firming up on the one thought ...'

'Which one?'

'That Clifford killed Joseph Rigby because he felt Rigby stepped out of line, doing his own thing.... Maybe it wasn't Clifford at all.'

Cardinal stopped his pacing and looked thoughtfully at Grout. 'But if so, who the hell should we be looking for?' His ascetic features mirrored the doubts that were plaguing his mind. Abruptly, he turned on his heel and marched towards the door, glancing at his watch. 'To hell with it. I've arranged to meet Carmela Cacciatore downstairs in the bar. Maybe she'll have more information for us. We can talk further, you and I, but we won't discuss it here. We'll do it downstairs, with our Italian temptress over a drink.'

Grout followed Cardinal out of the room. They took the lift down to the ground floor and as they entered the reception lounge, they were aware of a large number of men emerging from the open doors of the conference hall at the far end. The meeting was over, and the last stragglers were coming out of the lecture room. Cardinal scowled, guessing that it would make a drink at the bar difficult if not impossible to obtain among the crowd. He told Grout to return the key of Clifford's room to the receptionist while he went to the bar to meet Carmela.

She was already in the bar, seated against the far wall with a drink in front of her. The bar, surprisingly, was not as crowded as Cardinal had feared. Presumably the members of the conference had been provided with a separate, exclusive room for their refreshment.

Cardinal raised a hand in recognition, placed an order at the bar for a brandy and soda and walked across to the woman waiting for him. Carmela Cacciatore really was a beautiful woman, even dressed in a somewhat severe manner on this occasion. But the severity ended at her throat: the top of her white blouse was unbuttoned and he could see the first swell of her magnificent bosom. It would always be a little difficult to concentrate on business in the presence of this woman, Cardinal concluded.

'Any discoveries upstairs?' she asked him hopefully.

He shook his head, sat down beside her. 'Nothing. The room's as clean as a whistle. What about you?'

She considered for a few moments, then shrugged. 'The Carabinieri Art Squad has become a very efficient organization over the years. But apart from our own experts we, like other organizations, must deal from time to time with informants.' She smiled briefly. 'Like *Le Cochon*, for instance. It is not something I enjoy doing. I would prefer to lock such people away and make an end of it. But one must … temporize.' She sighed. 'However, with regard to our current business, the only thing I have been able to discover from my colleagues is that there are many rumours in the air. The dealers, the traders, the shady men who deal with the museums, they have begun to congregate here in Amsterdam.'

'Is there any talk of the Eagle of Milan?'

Carmela shook her head. 'Not specifically. The talk is only of an item of considerable value and historical interest. Beyond that, nothing. It is very strange, however. There is something almost *amateurish* about the whole thing. It is whispered that whoever is offering the artefact for sale is relatively new to the game. He – or she – is not one of the *cordata*, it may even be that this is his first foot in hot water.' She glanced at him quickly, smiled. 'That is an English idiom, is it not? I have expressed myself correctly in your language?'

Cardinal laughed. 'Close enough,' he said.

Someone was entering the bar. Cardinal looked up and raised a hand. Detective Sergeant Grout caught sight of him and nodded. He was not alone. Entering the bar with Grout was a tall, well-built, curly-headed man whose face was vaguely familiar to Cardinal. As the two men came forward Grout was smiling, but there was something else in his attitude that surprised Cardinal; he was aware of a certain veiled excitement in the detective sergeant's eyes.

The two newcomers stood in front of the table where Cardinal and Carmela sat. Grout's tone was cool, and controlled. He gestured to the man at his side. 'I've met an acquaintance from Newcastle! May I introduce you, sir?'

He touched the left arm of the smiling, handsome man with the frosted sideburns and the friendly eyes. 'This is Detective Chief Inspector Cardinal … and with him is Miss Carmela Cacciatore. May I introduce to you Professor Donald Godfrey of the University of Newcastle?'

CHAPTER TWELVE

G ODFREY UNCORKED THE bottle and poured himself a liberal glass of champagne, then did the same for Cardinal, Carmela and Grout. He grinned expansively at the others as the waiter walked away and he raised his glass. '*Salut!* This is a damned sight better than fighting for a drink in the conference bar.'

'And the surroundings are certainly comfortable,' Grout observed, glancing around the bar. 'But what exactly are we celebrating, Professor?'

'The end of a strenuous few days,' Godfrey replied. 'A successful end to my tour in Europe, a few days more, at leisure, and then I hope to be on my way again.'

'You celebrate in style, Professor,' Cardinal said quietly, eyeing Grout, slightly puzzled. Carmela sat without speaking, but her glance was fixed curiously on the new arrival.

'Ah, well,' Godfrey said carelessly, 'when I travel abroad I feel I ought to do it in comfort, you know? When I agree to give a talk I take my appropriate fee, but I also insist that my accommodation is not of the basic kind. If I'm not giving a talk but travelling under my own resources, well, after all, I have my university salary, my television earnings, my book royalties, and I'm single.' His glance flickered appreciatively towards Carmela, as though laying down a challenge. 'There's no reason why I shouldn't spend my money on life's little luxuries. No harm in looking after myself, hey?'

'No harm at all, sir,' Cardinal said coolly. 'But what exactly are you doing here in Amsterdam?'

Godfrey leaned back in his chair and crossed one leg over the other. He took a long sip at his drink and smiled. 'I'm in the middle of a lecture tour. It was planned about eight months ago, you know, though the itinerary wasn't finally decided until March. I've been to Rome, and Cologne, and this is the latest call in the whistle stop. Tomorrow, I'll have a rest day and then it's on to Norway, after which I head for the States—'

'Professor Godfrey is an expert in archaeology, and antiquities,' Grout explained to Carmela. He turned back to Godfrey. 'There's much interest in your topics on this lecture tour?'

'My audiences seem fascinated by them! Believe me, my dear chap, they can't get enough of it. The history of mediaeval England.' Godfrey grinned again, almost mischievously. A certain euphoria crept into his tone. 'I'm thinking of trying to con them in the States, persuade them into giving me a television series while I'm over there. Why today, in the audience I had downstairs, they were eighty per cent American tourists. And they lapped up what I had to say!' He laughed, suddenly self-deprecating. 'But there I go, blowing my own trumpet. Working in television does that for you ... makes you extrovert. But what are you two gentlemen doing in Amsterdam? You're a long way from home. And I can hardly believe you would be on holiday!'

Grout glanced at Cardinal and the flicker in his eyes told him to go ahead. 'We're really still making enquiries into that Rigby killing, up at Chesters Fort,' Grout said.

Professor Godfrey pursed his lips, widened his eyes. 'Really? The one you told me about when we met at the university? And it's brought you here to Amsterdam?'

'That's so. One thing's sort of led to another. But it seems we've now come up to a sort of dead end.' Grout sipped his champagne and watched Godfrey as he leaned forward in interest. 'A real dead end. The man who we'd hoped would help us in our enquiries has been murdered, you see. Chap called Kling.'

Godfrey pulled a face and managed a theatrical shudder. 'Not my idea of fun, chasing killers around Europe. Still, everyone to his trade, I suppose. And it gets you out of the house, if you know what I mean.' He turned to Carmela, gave her a well-honed, practised smile. 'And you also, *signorina*, you are with the police?'

'Not exactly.' Carmela's tone was sober. She was not smiling. 'I am … interested in antiques.'

'A collector? Interesting….'

'Not exactly,' she said with a slight smile. Then she added, 'But you, Professor Godfrey, I believe you're a collector of antiques?'

'How would you deduce that?' Godfrey asked, raising his neatly trimmed eyebrows.

'I believe I have seen one of your television appearances. When I was in London with my colleague, Mr Landon. I believe your collection is extensive.'

'I wouldn't say that, exactly.' The nonchalant smile on Godfrey's face was suddenly less nonchalant, stiffened at the edges. He shrugged, reluctantly. 'I suppose you could say it's … a collection of some consequence.'

'Built up over the years, no doubt.' Carmela nodded solemnly. 'But how does one pick up bargains as an amateur collector, you know, of expensive items?'

Godfrey frowned, seemed slightly offended at the term. *'Amateur*? Well, I suppose I may be so described, though my work as a professor in the Antiquities section of the university has given me certain acquired skills. That, and of course one develops a flair for these things, an eye, an instinct for picking up the right article at the right price—'

'But that means you must also be good at making the right contacts?' Cardinal intervened almost innocently. Carmela glanced at him, and at Grout. It was as though she had become aware of a rising tension in the group. There was something going on which she had not latched onto.

Godfrey hesitated before answering. 'What sort of contacts do you mean?'

Cardinal made no sign of replying and there was a sudden silence in the room. Carmela broke it by asking pleasantly, 'Do you not fear that from time to time items you pick up might be stolen property? Artefacts of doubtful provenance?'

Godfrey licked his lips and injected more life into his grin. 'Oh, not much chance of that if you deal with the right people, and it's pretty much a closed circle really. Of course, you won't know enough about the trade to—'

'That is not so,' Carmela replied quietly. Her eyes seemed to be searching him, as though calculating. 'Earlier, I was not ... what is the word ... explicit? When I said I was not of the police. In fact, I work for the Italian military.'

'Really? In what capacity?' Godfrey asked.

'I am a senior officer in the Carabinieri Art Squad. We investigate theft and the trade in illicit looted artefacts.'

There was a brief silence. Godfrey slowly finished his glass of champagne, laid it down. He glanced at his companions, raised an eyebrow, then topped up his glass. There was very little left in the bottle.

'Didn't I hear you were asked to show your collection on television?' Cardinal asked. 'You refused, didn't you? You didn't want the collection shown?'

'Yes, that's so ... Another glass of champagne? I could call for another bottle.'

Cardinal glanced at Grout, shook his head and refused. He spoke to Carmela. 'Interestingly enough, it was Professor Godfrey who first put us on the track of the Eagle of Milan.'

'Is that so?' Carmela asked, her eyes widening in surprise.

Godfrey frowned. 'The Eagle of Milan? Did I? I don't recall—'

'You've heard of it, of course.'

Godfrey sipped his champagne and made no immediate reply.

'Well, perhaps DCI Cardinal is overstating matters,' Grout said by way of explanation to Carmela. 'Professor Godfrey was sort of *instrumental* in the matter, since an interview with him led to my meeting a former student of his, Philip Proud.' He smiled at Godfrey. 'He spoke highly of you, for helping him get his degree.'

'It was the least I could do,' Godfrey muttered in a self-deprecating tone but he was clearly uneasy.

Grout stared at him coldly. 'I suppose it was ... in view of the fact that, in my view, you could well have had a hand in the disappearance of the manuscript.'

'*Me?*' A sudden chill seemed to descend in the room. There was a long silence. Godfrey sat stock still, opened his eyes wide and stared in bewilderment at Grout. Slowly his glance travelled to Cardinal, his expression showing amazement at what Grout had said. 'I beg your pardon? What are you trying to suggest? That I had anything to do with that tawdry business?

I was his *supervisor*! What possible motive would I have for such behaviour? Proud's thesis was destroyed in some student prank, a rag – even though there might have been some malicious intent behind it, some trouble over a woman—'

Carmela was frowning. 'I do not follow this discussion. What does this have to do with the flight of the Eagle?'

Cardinal waved a dismissive hand. He shrugged. 'Perhaps DS Grout is testing an hypothesis. Merely theorizing. But you see, *signorina*, we've reached an impasse in our investigation. There is a link missing. But I begin to see what my colleague is driving at. We need to go back to the beginning. Back, to trace the sequence of events that led to a murder in Northumberland, and ending here in Amsterdam with the murder of a man I've been hunting down for years. In which your Eagle of Milan seems to have played some kind of role.'

'So I'm to be made a stalking horse, a target, an excuse, for ridiculous accusations, just to get you out of an investigative difficulty?' Godfrey asked aggressively.

'Very good, very good, Professor Godfrey, a convincing challenge but let's not get too excited; Grout is raising a mere suggestion, and it may well have truth in it. But let's hear DS Grout out, shall we?'

'I would like that,' Carmela said quietly. 'I fear I still do not understand....'

'And I fail to see....' Godfrey began, but Grout cut in over him.

'Your presence here in Amsterdam, it's probably just a coincidence, of course, but it sets me off on a new train of thought, sets up a new kind of perspective for us. Let me explain.'

Cardinal was listening intently as Grout spoke.

'Professor, you indirectly led me to the thesis of Philip Proud. And now you're here on your lecture tour. Is it merely chance that the man we were looking for, Gus Clifford, was also here? Waiting for a meeting? And Signorina Cacciatore, she tells us there are rumours in the air. Representatives of the museums are gathering. Here in Amsterdam. Some of them, she tells us, are, shall we say … somewhat shady. Working on the fringe of illegality. But it's as though there might be a kind of auction going on. Something Clifford would not have wanted. But then, he's dead now.

'So let's recap. Clifford was here, the Carabinieri Art Squad informants talk about some kind of important sale … and here we also have the man who supervised Philip Proud's thesis, which the dead man at Chesters, Rigby, inspected – and which we think led to violence in the search for a long lost artefact: the Eagle brooch of the Duke of Milan. Oh, and there is also the coincidental fact that you yourself are a collector of ancient artefacts….'

Godfrey shook his head in disdain. 'This seems to me a mish-mash of supposition, a series of coincidences and unrelated facts – and what you seem to be seeking to tie me into I don't understand. I'm on a lecture tour, damn it, and that's all!'

There was a short, constrained silence. Then Carmela spoke. 'You are a private collector who does not wish to expose his collection to the world. I think at some time I would like to inspect your collection, Professor Godfrey.'

'It's a *private* collection!' he spat angrily. 'I've simply never wanted publicity!'

'That is what many private collectors say,' she advised, 'when they have something to hide.'

'Particularly if the collection contains an important artefact … like the Eagle of the Duke of Milan,' Grout added. He glanced at DCI Cardinal who raised an eyebrow, in silent assent. 'Let me try to explain the way I'm thinking, Professor

Godfrey. You see, we've been proceeding on the assumption that it was the antiques looter Gus Clifford who killed his associate Rigby. I'm largely to blame for that. I *wanted* it to be Clifford. The chief inspector also wanted it to be Clifford, he's been chasing him for years. We wanted to pin the Rigby killing on him. Oh, we're pretty sure he killed Rigby's mistress in Sheffield all right, but my guess is that Clifford sought out this woman just to find out what Rigby was doing at Chesters. He found out, and then killed her to shut her up. Then he went after what Rigby himself had been after ... the same thing, I wonder, the same thing *you* had been after in the first instance.'

There was a strained silence in the room now as Cardinal said quietly. 'You're talking about the Eagle brooch of the Duke of Milan.'

The professor was keeping his emotions under control. 'I haven't the faintest idea what you're talking about. I've heard vaguely the story of the Eagle's disappearance—' Godfrey said with the air of a completely surprised man, but Grout interrupted him again.

'*Vaguely*? But you supervised Proud's thesis! It won't wash, Professor,' Grout said. 'DCI Cardinal and I, we've not had a chance to really discuss this, but I can now see where we went wrong in the beginning, and once we look back to the start of it, both of us could well come to the same conclusion, independently, even if all the pieces don't yet fit into place.'

'It's still largely guesswork, of course,' Cardinal said carefully.

'But even if I say so myself, sir, it's logical and intelligent guesswork,' Grout insisted. 'The fact is, on a more wide-ranging view of things, seeing the professor here, apparently innocently, after our recent experiences, I get the feeling that if we were to check through his collection of antiques I bet we'd find some stuff that's of doubtful provenance. That's probably why he was reluctant to have his collection displayed on television. After all, one would expect the professor would normally welcome such exposure. But he turned down the chance. I can guess why...' He watched Godfrey carefully, waiting for a reaction. 'Where did you get some of your stuff from? Joseph Rigby? *Le Cochon*? Some of the other dealers who are familiar to Signorina Cacciatore? We'll soon find out if they have had dealings with you. Now there's been a murder involved, they'll be keen to talk, to make a deal.... We don't know how or when you made your contacts but we'll find out.'

Godfrey remained silent, but his fingers were rigid as they grasped the glass in his hands.

'I think your mistake, of course, was to let Rigby know too much. What happened? Did you approach him to break into Chesters Fort?'

'Dear me, gentlemen, this really is—'

'Uncomfortable? Oh come off it, Godfrey.' Cardinal's tone was suddenly harsh. 'I'm with Grout on this. You read that thesis of Proud's, you linked its finding with your own research and you guessed that the brooch stolen from Lodovico Sforza had eventually ended up in Chesters Fort.'

'Probably cemented inside that legionary statue,' Grout supplied, 'where it had been hidden by Simon Bollands. You wanted it, you decided to ask Rigby to get it for you, not immediately, but near the time you planned your lecture tour. Because you wanted to take it into Europe, to fence it. It would be too big a prize for your own collection, but it would give you a huge financial boost ... and it would make you rich.'

Godfrey finished his glass of champagne, but there was a slight tremor in his hand as Grout went on. 'The trouble was

Rigby got interested; you probably told him too much. His curiosity was aroused and he went to Proud, read the thesis for himself and got the message it contained. You learned of the visit and knew you'd better cover tracks in case others cottoned on, so you broke into Proud's flat and destroyed the thesis in case Rigby, or others, got their hands on it. You didn't want anyone else to see what it contained.'

'We appreciate,' Cardinal said sarcastically, 'that you had to support his degree award thereafter. Otherwise, he might have been forced to rewrite it, or could have pressed for a closer investigation into its destruction.'

Godfrey began to rise to his feet. 'I think this farce has gone far enough,' he said thickly.

'No farce,' Grout said. 'And you were far from laughing when you realized Rigby was after the legionary piece. Did you follow him out to Chesters Fort that night? Or maybe you went together. Whichever way it was, when he came out of the museum my guess is he told you he was keeping the statue, and what it contained. So you killed him.'

Godfrey stood staring at them. 'I'm a bloody academic, not a killer,' he snarled. 'This is ridiculous. You're making a mistake. This man Clifford you mentioned, I know nothing of him … all this other nonsense is fanciful.'

'Clifford didn't kill Rigby,' Cardinal said, nodding to himself. 'He couldn't have done it. The time factor was against him. He'd called a meeting in London; he only cancelled it when he learned Rigby wasn't coming. By that time Rigby was already heading for Chesters.'

'Where *you* killed him,' Grout murmured, glowering at Professor Godfrey.

'As for Clifford, he didn't even *know* about the da Vinci brooch at that stage. He didn't know why Rigby had died.'

219

Cardinal glanced at Grout as he caught the hint of anger in his voice. 'He went after Eloise Parker to find out what it was all about and she told him about the jewel. So he rewarded her by strangling her and then he left the country. He came after you.'

'If this man Clifford was after me,' Godfrey sneered, 'why didn't he turn up at Cologne?'

'Why should he?' Cardinal spoke reasonably, still pleased with himself. 'After all, you'd used your lecture tour to cover your auction of the brooch ... I doubt if you were reckless enough to bring it with you but here in Amsterdam, you could make use of the gathering of predatory museum suppliers to seek a deal... But Clifford was hovering too and finally guessed there'd be no need to face you until you came here, to Amsterdam. Where he could dispose of it.'

'To a gentleman called *Le Cochon,*' Grout added, 'who was quite disposed to help us once he learned Clifford was dead. We were puzzled, you see, as to why Clifford waited in his villa, then came here and again delayed. Now we know why. He was waiting for you to arrive. Once you were on your way, he flew to Amsterdam. And that's when you were lucky.'

Godfrey lit a cigarette. If his confidence was draining away he showed no evidence of it. His hand was steady; he was still very much in control of his nerves. 'All right,' he said calmly, 'I'll go along with your little charade. Tell me, just how am I supposed to be *lucky* at this juncture?'

'It's my guess,' Grout said, 'that Clifford intended meeting you with another man. A man called Schneider. He came ahead to fix a meeting with *Le Cochon.* Schneider was to come later so they would not openly travel together. But when he met you, Schneider was to be there.'

Godfrey laughed, somewhat raggedly. 'This fellow Schneider ... what part was he supposed to play in this—'

'He was to kill you, after you'd made the brooch available to Clifford.'

The laugh died abruptly, and Godfrey stared at Grout then drew quickly on his cigarette. 'You say I was lucky.'

'That's right. Because we got to the villa on the Bodensee before Schneider left.' Grout hesitated, then went on, 'I … I tangled with Schneider. He came off worst. The consequence was he just didn't turn up in Amsterdam. So Clifford sought a meeting with you, without Schneider.'

'And?'

Cardinal smiled thinly. 'Time for you to talk to us. You tell us.'

Godfrey stared at him seriously. His broad handsome face expressed a certain disdain as he said, 'I've got nothing to say. You two are the ones addicted to fairy tales. I've nothing to add to this romancing.'

'No matter,' Cardinal shrugged. 'We can make guesses. Any other suppositions, Grout?'

The detective sergeant kept his eyes fixed on Godfrey. 'I think Clifford took a room in this hotel because he knew Godfrey would be here. I think that at some time last night he either broke into this room and searched it for the jewel or otherwise faced Godfrey and demanded it, threatening him with exposure or perhaps death. Either way, it ended with Godfrey striking him down, from behind, of course. As he did Rigby, at Chesters. *Modus operandi.*'

'A professor of history overcoming a professional criminal? Really…' Godfrey began to laugh but there was a false note to it.

Quietly, Grout said, 'We've already seen an example of your nerve this evening, Professor. You've faced us with complete calm, most of the time.'

'Because I've nothing to hide.'

'You're a good actor, Professor,' Grout continued. 'You're used to an audience, at university, on television. You're controlled. I don't think you'd have found difficulty in convincing Clifford you were scared, or submissive, or under his control. And when he relaxed, you struck him.'

'This is all a lot of nonsense.'

'The city would be quiet enough in the early hours,' Cardinal said. 'It wouldn't be difficult for a big man like you to haul an unconscious man back to the car he had hired. You could have placed him in the passenger seat, driven him to the Amstel, and ... there he was. Dead in the car you pushed into the canal. Out of your way. And with no connection between the two of you, apparently.'

Godfrey breathed deeply and stubbed out his cigarette with fierce, controlled jab. 'Or in *reality*. But that's the point, isn't it?' he said. 'That's the crux of the whole matter. There is no real connection between this Clifford and me. All you've said is nothing more than supposition, wild guesswork.'

'Agreed,' Cardinal said calmly.

Godfrey laughed, some of the confidence leaching back into his tone. He stood up, reaching his full height and his ease of manner seemed to grow also. 'There's also another matter. This isn't England. Even if you could prove I'd done all you say, you have no jurisdiction over me. I can walk out of here at any time, free as a bird.'

'Correction,' Cardinal said. 'You could *try*. But take the sergeant here. He's a big chap. Maybe he'd stop you. Illegal, yes, but in a good cause. Besides, where could you run? We'd be on to you within minutes. I only have to make one phone call and I'd have the immediate co-operation of Interpol, the German, Austrian and Dutch police. They're already working with us.

We can get them to serve a European Arrest Warrant. The fact is, Professor Godfrey, you're stymied. You haven't a chance. You've a lot of questions to answer. We'll be looking at your collection. And at your recent movements. We'll be talking to the dealers who've congregated here in Amsterdam. And to Carmela's informants. And who knows what will turn up in due course, when we take a close forensic look at Clifford? Will we find his prints in your room? Will we find traces of you in the car in which he died? Who knows? Who knows what will turn up to trap you?'

Godfrey stared at the two police officers. His face was expressionless. 'You still can't get over the basic problem. You said yourself ... all this is guesswork, supposition. You can't prove a damn thing.'

Cardinal finished his drink, climbed awkwardly to his feet and looked around the room with a self-satisfied air. 'You know, Professor, I'm just a plodding jack, that's all. And the kind of dogged, detailed work we now need to do is right up my street. And as we've said, who knows what we'll find?'

Godfrey seemed turned to stone. In a hoarse voice he said, 'You'll never be able to prove all this. You'll never pin it on me.'

Grout smiled. 'We think otherwise. Then ... well, we'll just have to see, won't we?'

Carmela Cacciatore rose to her feet. There was an excited light in her eyes. 'After all these years....' she murmured. She turned a dazzling smile upon Professor Godfrey. 'I have found this discussion most interesting. My colleague Arnold Landon is presently in Northumberland. I will contact him immediately. We have good relationships with the Northumberland police. I will advise him to immediately seek their assistance, in a search of your premises, to create a catalogue of your private collection of artefacts, check upon the provenance of all such articles. It's likely what we seek – Beatrice's da Vinci brooch so beloved by the Duke of Milan – may well be elsewhere, a bank deposit box perhaps? Who knows? But my colleagues in the Carabinieri Art Squad, they have much expertise in such matters.'

She smiled at Grout and Cardinal. 'To you, gentlemen, I will of course leave the question of murders ... but my colleagues and I will look for the brooch designed by da Vinci for Lodovico Sforza, the Duke of Milan. And I feel certain we will find it.'

She edged past them, heading for the door. Over her shoulder, she said, 'And then the long flight of the Eagle will at last be over....'